Bolan's steel eyes slashed at the enemy

Emilia Salerno executed a fast draw that cleared the Scorpion from its holster. Her pasty face twisted in hatred as she hurled abuse at Mack Bolan.

The Executioner moved like lightning.

Slugs flattened the woman against the wall, her oozing wounds smearing the wallpaper with gobs of blood. She took one, two stumbling steps toward Bolan.

Then she dropped. Dead. Gone was one of the most ruthless terrorists Mack Bolan had yet encountered.

But his troubles had just begun.

"America's most successful adventure series. The best in the business."

—*Navy News*

Also available from Gold Eagle Books,
publishers of the Executioner series:

Mack Bolan's
ABLE TEAM

Mack Bolan's
PHOENIX FORCE

MACK BOLAN

THE EXECUTIONER 52

BOLAN

Tuscany Terror

A GOLD EAGLE BOOK FROM

W☷RLDWIDE

TORONTO · NEW YORK · LONDON

First edition April 1983

ISBN 0-373-61052-1

Special thanks and acknowledgment to
Stephen Mertz for his contributions to this work.

Printed in Canada

"There is an American hidden in the soil of every
country and in the soul of every people."
                                    —*Eric Hoffer*

"We do all stand in the front ranks of the battle
every moment of our lives; where there is a brave man
there is the thickest of the fight,
and there the post of honor."
                            —*Henry David Thoreau*

"I am an American, but I am by no means at the
center of every brave struggle in the world.
It is just that Americans are a primary target of
terror today, and I have no choice but to bust in
and make damn near every fight my own."
                        —*Mack Bolan, The Executioner*
                        (from his journal)

The Stony Man War-Room Team

of Mack Samuel Bolan, alias John Macklin Phoenix, retired Colonel, U.S.A., known as The Executioner a.k.a. Kicker, Striker, Stony Man One:

April Rose, primary mission controller and overseer of Stony Man's Virginia "Farm" HQ. Provides logistics, back-up support, loving care for the Phoenix people. Tall, lush-bodied, this shapely lady has been Mack Bolan's closest ally since The Executioner's final Days of De-Creation.

Hal Brognola, director of the Sensitive Operations Group, Stony Man liaison with the Oval Office. In his three-piece suit this ex-FBI agent looks like a vice-president of IBM. In fact he is a street-wise third-generation American who worked his own way into the stratosphere of the Justice Department's covert operations section. In that capacity he first met Mack Bolan. The rest is history.

Andrzej Konzaki, officially with Special Weapons Development, CIA, is unofficially attached to the Phoenix program. One of the most innovative armorers in the world. Master weaponsmith, expert on small arms, handguns to machine guns; knives; small explosives; other devices; and assigns them according to circumstances, locales. Legless since Vietnam. His CIA profile says: "Trust him."

Aaron "The Bear" Kurtzman, big, rumpled librarian of Stony Man's extensive electronic data bank, from which he interfaces with those of the National Security Council, the Justice Department, the CIA,

DIA and the intelligence agencies of every allied nation. Brilliant, a living extension of his computer. His tobacco-stained fingers dance over the console to call up mug shots, maps, raw data of all kinds.

Leo Turrin, Mob elder statesman (Leo "The Pussy" Turrin), undercover agent for Justice's Orgcrime Division, Washington lobbyist with connections, now officer of the Phoenix operation. From a *capo* on *La Commissione* to special friend and advisor to Bolan the blitz artist, this lieutenant of both the international underworld and sensitive operations walks a perilous path through the savage pastures.

Jack Grimaldi, combat pilot in Nam (137 missions, 2 Purple Hearts), later a flyboy for the Mob, now head of his own SOG cadre: G-Force. Can fly anything from a single-engine Scout to a Boeing 767, has proven himself to be Bolan's ace card on many missions. Of Italian parentage, is flamboyant, reckless, yet ruthlessly efficient. King of the sky.

Plus Tommy Anders, Toby Ranger, Smiley Dublin and others who are in constant touch with Stony Man's War Room, as are Mack Bolan's two tactical neutralization teams, Phoenix Force and Able Team.

The Phoenix program is a covert operation, unrecorded in the official records. Full U.S. government support makes the 160-acre Stony Man estate in the Shenandoah mountains the command center of the most formidable national security force ever assembled.

Dedicated to those good people of every race
who understand that no evil is greater than
believing that one race of people
is more or less evil than another.

PROLOGUE

MACK BOLAN. WARRIOR. FIGHTER. DEFENDER.

No. Not defender. Mack Bolan did not have it in him to sit back passively and wait for the enemy to seek him out. The enemy had enough advantages already.

The best defense was a strong attack. Seek out the enemy and hit him first. Hit him when he wasn't ready for you. Hit him hard. Hit him again and again. And be as merciless to him as he was to his victims.

That philosophy was basic to Mack Bolan's strategy and to his tactics as well. Everything was designed around it. The whole of Stony Man Farm—information, communications, weaponry, transport—all of it had only one purpose: to enable the world warrior to carry out his missions faster than fast, and with the utmost efficiency.

It was how Mack Bolan, single-handed at first, raw out of Vietnam, had been able to take on the huge organization that was the Mafia—and to defeat it, time after time. Later he had added friends—

dedicated, loyal friends—and the war against the *mafiosi* roared into high gear.

Now that person called Mack Bolan was ostensibly dead, burned alive in the explosion of his famed War Wagon in Central Park. A scorched body had been found in it. Mack Bolan? Well, that's what they said.

So Bolan was officially and legally dead—but another identity had been provided to take his place.

If anyone checked the records in the Department of Defense, there was a full and complete\file on a man called John Phoenix from the time he was born, through grade school and high school, his appointment to the military academy at West Point by his local congressman, his graduation in the upper third of his class, and his complete service record from the time he was sworn in as a second lieutenant, infantry, to his retirement as a full colonel.

John Phoenix was entitled to wear the insignia of matched eagles on his shoulder and collar tabs. An American eagle was a fitting symbol for the identity that Mack Bolan had taken on when he agreed to give up his original identity and wage war against a new enemy—international terrorism.

A few close comrades still knew him as Mack Bolan, and, in private, called him by that name. But to the world of the military, the police, the government and the press, it was different. To them, the lean, hard, icy-eyed fighter was known as John

Phoenix, ex-infantry officer, and it was as John Phoenix that the big guy went out to fight.

He did not go out to play games. Therefore he was invariably at odds with the government that had, in effect, joined his kind of war.

Government policy dictated that international incidents be avoided unless all else failed. In reality, aggressors deserved to be hit the moment their intentions were made known. But politics and propaganda sometimes—often—interfered with direct action, creating tangle upon tangle of confusion and frustration. This then led to widespread conditions of nervous caution that approached a paranoid proportion.

Such a situation created a very real fear of being, accidentally, the first to make a false move.

No, Mack Bolan did not like those kinds of restrictions, however well-intentioned the cautionary "policies" were. Indeed, the path to hell was paved with the damn things. It wasn't a path to hell anymore, either. It was a goddamn superhighway.

So when John Phoenix went out to fight, he went out to *fight*!

1

THE INFORMER WAS LATE.

Bolan stood in the deep shadow of a doorway.

A breeze from Switzerland sliced across Lake Como from the north. An icy chill bit into the darkness.

The town of Como, in northern Italy, is a bustling tourist spa etched into the Alps at the southern tip of the lake.

Now Como silently slept.

During the day, this stretch of medieval street was clogged with traffic. But in the early morning, the street belonged to the darkness, to Bolan.

The cathedral of Santa Maria Maggiore, a magnificent stone structure of fourteenth-century Gothic architecture, towered over him. A distant streetlight cast a sinister air on the cathedral's finely carved main entrance.

Bolan was clad in jacket, sweater and slacks, the norm for casual wear in a vacation center like Como. The clothing's dark colors helped him blend into the shadows that bordered the deserted street.

Bolan wore a silenced Beretta 93-R—his new auto-pistol—equipped with an oversize trigger guard and a fold-down grip for a two-handed hold. Because of its compactness, the sixteen-round automatic hung in custom-lengthened leather under his left arm, a bulge beneath his jacket.

He was in his element, alone with the night, alone with the wind that cut through the streets and disturbed the calm.

One thought hammered in his mind.

The informer was late.

In the world and wars of the Executioner, the briefest delay could be the difference between success and failure.

Success, in this mission, meant the rescue and assured safety of two kidnapped American citizens: a thirty-two-year-old mother and her three-year-old daughter.

Failure could be translated as death, grizzly death. If Bolan failed, the two Americans would be slaughtered.

The mother and her child had already suffered agonies of the damned. Anger at those agonies clawed at Mack Bolan's gut.

He would make the terror merchants pay for those bastard deeds. Yeah.

The informer was a loose-lipped member of Italy's terrorist mob, the Red Justice Column.

It was the Red Column that had claimed responsibility for the kidnapping of Louise DiAlto and her little daughter, Angel.

Bolan was in Italy to rescue the two Americans. And destroy the Red Justice Column.

He was up to his neck in a hell that stemmed from a distant blood tie of a good American soldier, Mike DiAlto.

It was because DiAlto was a three-times-removed cousin of a long-dead Mafia boss, Charlie "Lucky" Luciano, that DiAlto's wife and child had been kidnapped.

DiAlto was in a severe bind. So was NATO. And Mack Bolan was in the front lines once more, in the hellgrounds that smolder with horror, endless betrayal, death.

Bolan had studied Colonel DiAlto's Army 201 file on the flight to Italy. DiAlto was a veteran Army man. Bolan felt almost a blood-brother kinship with the guy, though they had met only once, spending about twenty minutes together back in Milan—where DiAlto and a few others were nervously awaiting word from the Executioner.

Mike DiAlto had brought honor upon himself and the men of his outfit as a captain of infantry during two tours of combat duty in Vietnam. He was now an aide to the chief of staff for logistics and administration in NATO's Southern Command, stationed in Verona.

DiAlto, a third generation Italian-American who

spoke Italian like a native, was also the chief American liaison officer to the Italian government's antiterrorist squad, the Central Operative Nucleus for Security *(Nucleo Operativo Centrale di Sicurezza)*, known by its Italian acronym, NOCS.

DiAlto had been at this post for eight years. He was good at his job. He was a pro. Few people knew and no one cared that he was distantly related to a long-dead *capo* of the American Mafia.

No one, that is, until the Red Justice Column stormed into DiAlto's life.

The Red Column terrorists, since their emergence fifteen years earlier, had disrupted Italy and pushed the country to the brink of anarchy, contributing to the turmoil and muck of the nation's political life and claiming credit for nearly three hundred bloody terrorist attacks in a single year. The Red Column's motto was: *Mai senza Fucile*: Never without a Gun. The organization, made up of hard-core felons recruited as "liberation fighters," operated with the classic terrorist aim—to force the downfall of an established government by encouraging such stern measures to control their acts of violence that the population eventually revolts against that government. A sick trick, and a bloody one, and for all the ferocious murdering that went on, it never worked. It wasn't worth diddly-shit. But, yeah, they had plenty of guns.

The Red Column now waged war against the entire Atlantic alliance.

The terrorist group's goal was to get the despised Americans out of Italy and to get Italy out of NATO.

The Red Column had already tried to strangle the credibility of the American Command with a vicious whisper campaign. The false rumors said that Colonel DiAlto was a stooge for the Italian Mafia. With his Italian background, they thought he would be an easy target for such slanderous attacks.

NATO installations throughout Italy had remained on high security alert since the 1982 terrorist abduction of NATO's Brig. Gen. James Dozier. But the Red Column was powerful. The Red Column had penetrated that security and had gotten to DiAlto's family, spiriting Louise and Angel away during a shopping trip in downtown Verona.

The terrorists were demanding that DiAlto appear on Italian television and confess that he was a Mafia tool, a puppet directly linked to international organized crime—and, furthermore, that his superiors in Washington had sent him to Italy *because* of his Mafia connections.

To secure the release of his family, DiAlto was instructed to tell the world that he had been working with the Italian mob in the rape of Italian society.

For the first time ever, terrorists did not want the media to know of their involvement. Such knowledge would destroy the credibility of DiAlto's confession. Thus far, the Italian police and NATO had obeyed the demand to keep the lid on. If they disobeyed that order or if a leak occurred, two innocent Americans would be ruthlessly wasted.

A flurry of transatlantic telephone conferences between the American and Italian governments had resulted in a decision: the Italians would mount intensive police pressure while making room for a covert U.S. response.

Enter Mack Bolan, a.k.a. Colonel John Phoenix.

It was a situation plastered with urgency, and Bolan had been airlifted to the scene.

The U.S. response, like Bolan's, was emotional and direct: not another damned humiliation at the hands of terrorists; concern for the two victimized Americans; and the grim realization that such a gunpoint confession would have a tremendous effect on impressionable minds—it would be scored a propaganda victory at the very least and a political disaster for Italy and her NATO allies for a certainty.

Add pressure to the package. Time was running out.

DiAlto had already exceeded one deadline. The terrorists had given him until noon the following day to make his public confession or his wife and child would be slain.

As a reminder that no further deadlines should be missed, the terrorists had sent DiAlto a box containing a hacked-off human finger on a piece of bloodsplotched cotton. DiAlto had recognized the ring on the severed finger right away. He had purchased that ring; it was his wife's wedding band.

Bolan felt a sudden chill at the base of his spine. It was not from the cutting wind off the lake. A shuffling figure had materialized on the street.

It was the informer, Ciucci. Bolan knew it because he had been given a head-to-toe description of the kid. This guy matched it perfectly. The figure ambled through a pool of light cast by a streetlight, and Bolan surveyed him closely.

Ciucci looked and dressed exactly like the punk he was: a dropout, a twenty-year-old jerk from the Balduina student section of Rome. Ciucci was not the first, nor would he be the last bored kid of his generation.

Ferdinando Ciucci was now pissed off with his brief career as a go-fer for the Red Column. That was the reason he gave for offering to sell out his comrades once the rumors of the massive police hunt had reached him. The authorities wanted information. He had that information and for a price he would exchange it. The punk wanted ten thousand U.S. dollars. In return he would divulge the whereabouts of Louise and Angel.

Bolan brought no payoff money to this rendezvous. The big guy did not negotiate with terrorists. The information came free, or else. . . .

Ciucci would not be aware of this fact.

The informant hugged the shadows. He walked toward the statue of Pliny the Elder. Once he reached its base he stopped.

Bolan stayed put.

The kid looked around in the darkness. He was nervously kicking the ground, working himself into mounting panic.

Bolan was supposed to meet Ciucci at the base of that statue, but he remained in the sniper-shoadows of the doorway for a full two minutes, assuring himself that no one was trailing the kid on foot.

Bolan quit the shadows. He crossed the street, walking toward Ciucci, toward the answer to where two U.S. citizens were being held and tortured. He made no secret of his approach, and he did not lower his guard.

But he sensed a trap.

Ferdinando Ciucci saw Bolan coming. The kid was unkempt, clad in shabby jeans, T-shirt and jacket. Watching the big guy approach did nothing for the punk's nerves. He backpedaled a few steps until the marble base of Pliny the Elder forced him to halt.

"Relax," Bolan growled in English from ten paces away. It was not a statement, it was an order. "I'm the guy you're looking for."

The kid hesitated for a second. "*Signor* . . . I want to go somewhere else . . . before we talk."

Before Bolan could respond, the trap was sprung.

Piercing headlights razored a gash through the night, freezing Bolan and Ciucci in their glare. A dark Fiat squealed onto the street and was racing toward them.

Ciucci was petrified, glued to the spot as if hypnotized by the headlights.

Bolan dived at the kid. His right hand yanked the Beretta from its shoulder holster as his left arm reached out and knocked Ciucci to the pavement with him as the Fiat roared past. A machine gun was blazing from the car's window.

Bolan and Ciucci crashed to the pavement. Bolan continued in a roll away from the kid, coming back up several feet away. He trusted Ciucci to keep down out of the line of fire.

The punk could not be trusted to do anything. Screaming like a madman, Ciucci scrambled to his feet, his instincts short-circuiting under the pressure of the machine-gun fire.

The machine gun never stopped firing.

The ancient street reverberated with its thunder.

Mack Bolan was out of his roll and moving in a low crouch, the Beretta tracking up on the Fiat—just in time to see Ciucci stop his screaming. Forever.

The steady hail of weaponfire stitched the informer, splashing the night with blood and spinning the terrorist fink in a death jig that ended in a sprawl to the pavement.

Bolan's only solid clue was blown away.

But the killers were not finished yet; they had their sights set on another kill. They tracked Bolan.

2

IN THE BLINKING OF AN EYE, the machine gunner in the Fiat lifted his firing finger from the trigger and swung the muzzle in Bolan's direction.

During those fumbling microseconds, the Executioner sighted his own weapon on the open side window of the coasting car. He steadied his aim with a two-handed grip. The silenced Beretta sneezed hot death.

Bolan heard the *slap-suck* of a 9mm bullet hitting headbone. There was violent movement and a short tortured scream inside the Fiat. A weapon clattered to the pavement from the car's window. The machine gun was silent.

The driver of the car floored the gas pedal.

Bolan sighted on the car from a straight-armed stance. The Fiat rocketed up the dark street toward the next street corner.

He held his fire momentarily until the car crossed a stream of light from a streetlamp. Then he squeezed off a round at the Fiat's right rear tire. He wanted a living, talking prisoner. He wanted a lead.

He was rewarded. The tire exploded.

The car went into a wounded skid. It jumped the curb and tackled a trash bin before slamming into a lamppost in a metal-wrenching halt.

By the light of the streetlamp, Bolan could see the front door of the driver's side open. A guy wearing commando black crawled out.

Bolan knew the terrorist driver would be invisible once he left that patch of light.

The Executioner brought up the automatic and tracked toward the driver. With his aim set on a disabling leg hit, he fired a single shot, dropping the hardguy to the ground in an agonized scream. The driver was going nowhere now unless he crawled.

Bolan spun around and saw a second Fiat racing toward him, another free-firing machine gunner spitting flame from the car's open window. A sheet of slugs ricocheted off the cathedral steps to Bolan's left. The terrorists and the machine-gun fire were gaining on him.

Bolan propelled himself in a dive to his right, split heartbeats before whistling projectiles ripped a tight pattern where he had just been.

He hit the pavement and rolled. Regaining his feet, he dodged behind the rectangular base of the statue in front of the cathedral steps.

A dozen or more rounds zipped off the statue, zinging by Bolan's head.

The big guy had had enough. He emerged blazing,

hitting the back-up car, sending up a spray of splintered glass from the shattered rear window. He heard a scream, two screams.

Bolan needed the second car the hell out of the way so that he could talk to the leg-wounded driver of the first car.

And he got what he wanted. The driver screeched through a turn. The car disappeared.

Gone to lick fresh wounds, Bolan guessed, as he sprinted toward the driver of the crashed vehicle.

The man was lying on the pavement a few yards from the Fiat. He had obviously tried to crawl away into the darkness of the shadows, but had failed. Managing to crawl when pain seared the mind was something only men with guts could do. Scum like this man did not have those guts.

A puddle of blood, growing in size, surrounded the driver. He was bleeding from the leg and from the forehead, where he wore a large gash earned when his car crashed into the lamppost.

Bolan leaned over the man, grabbed a handful of jacket and yanked him up into a sitting position.

"You're beat," Bolan said, making each word distinct enough to stab through the guy's descending veil of pain. "The game's over," he said, shaking the guy. "Tell me where Louise DiAlto is. Now."

The man looked up into Bolan's hard eyes. Bolan returned the stare. The man shuddered.

"I don't know."

Bolan took out a negotiating device—the Beretta. He pointed it at the man's temple.

"Be a man, you bastard," Bolan calmly said. "A woman. A child. They're innocent." He put power to the point by pressing the muzzle of the Beretta against the terrorist's skull.

The man took a deep breath. "Savasta...Bellagio—" But his words were severed by the sound of tires gripping a corner.

Bolan legged it to the cover of a doorway, flattening himself against a wall in the shadows. The oncoming car was the second Fiat, back for a return engagement. Back for round two.

The car sped to the point where the previous firefight had taken place. As it approached, a terrorist opened fire on his own kind, on his wounded comrade.

The victim had seen his fellow guncocks coming and had shouted greetings, believing his life was saved. But it was not.

Wanting no excess baggage, especially injured baggage, the terrorists wiped out their comrade, stitching the man up and down with machine-gun fire.

His body rippled in a spasm of death.

The backup team's Fiat roared down the street in search of the big guy.

Bolan emerged from the shadows for a flash of time, just long enough to set his sights on the driver. The driver had been pummeled with the glass from the back window of the car, but that had not stopped him or his machine-gunning buddy. The Executioner would give them something a little more solid—that would stop them dead.

Aiming the Beretta, the big guy fired a round through the open back window. He knew he had connected. The windshield collapsed around the driver's ruptured face as the bullet exited his head.

The Fiat veered off the road. Speeding up and over the curb, the car became an airborne iron box. Then it became a fixture in a furniture shop as it dive-bombed into the store, crashing through the huge plate-glass window.

Two down, one to go.

Bolan knew the man on the streetside was dead, he knew the driver of the second car was dead, but he had a strong hunch that the machine gunner in the second Fiat was alive, if not well. Sailing through a furniture-store window would not necessarily spell the end.

Like a cat pawing through the night, Bolan silently padded his way toward the furniture store. Glass littered the sidewalk. Sirens littered the air as the town of Como came to life in the wake of the noise and the terror.

Bolan knew his time was short. The authorities would arrive on the scene soon, and they would want answers—if they could even begin to figure out the questions that were strewed among the mess. The big guy did not intend to be in the line of fire of those questions. He had done enough dodging for one night.

Bolan cautiously peered around the edge of the shattered window in time to see a dazed terrorist staggering out of the mangled car. The guy, wonderment pasted in his eyes, made only one mistake. He stood to shake the fog from his head and left his machine gun on the seat of the car. The guy never had a chance.

Bolan stared at him. The terrorist looked up, sensing he was being watched, and his eyes met the steel of Bolan's stare. The terrorist began babbling incoherently in Italian. The Executioner put him away.

The terrorist caught the bullet square in the forehead. Turning away, Bolan took off into the night, away from the sirens.

THE BIG GUY RACED DOWN EMPTY STREETS. Finally, after a long stretch, he found a telephone. He checked into the booth and dialed the number in Milan where the others were waiting.

Colonel DiAlto answered the phone on the first ring.

"Go ahead, Colonel Phoenix," he said. "We have a scrambler."

"It went sour," Bolan said with disgust. "Ciucci is dead. Four terrorists are dead, but one left me with two words, Bellagio and Savasta. Bellagio is a town

about twenty klicks from here, right? Savasta...
that's got to be a person or a place or something near
Bellagio.''

"Savasta. Got it. I'll run a tracer."

Bolan appreciated the strong, stoic front that
DiAlto was putting up. But the big guy easily read the
tension and strain in the NATO man's voice. He did
not blame DiAlto one bit—the man had his whole
world at stake.

"I'm leaving for Bellagio now," Bolan said.
"Contact me."

"Good luck, Colonel," DiAlto said.

Bolan broke the connection.

In the dark streets of Como, an Italian bloodbath
had begun. One sure bet, Bolan knew, was that more
blood would be spilled before it was over.

3

AARON "THE BEAR" KURTZMAN'S bulky form filled
the swivel chair in the computer room at Stony Man
Farm. His fingers lightly touched the keys of a CRT
terminal. His eyes were intently focused on the screen
as he watched the cursor lead the way, green word by
green word, line by line, across the display area. The
screen emitted a ghostly glare and a gold mine of information.

This was the Bear's lair. The level of the floor was
somewhat higher than surrounding rooms to accommodate the thick, high-powered cables that ran beneath it. Reels of magnetic tape revolved in sporadic
jabs on the central processing unit as they inter-
blocked, reading in and accessing data. The surface
of the walls and ceiling were specially tiled to dis-
sipate heat. Controlled streams of air filtered into the
sterile room to maintain an exact degree of coolness.
Uncarpeted floors ensured the absence of unwanted
electrical impulses created by static electricity.

Kurtzman protected himself from the chill with his
own excess weight plus layers of rumpled clothing

and a white lab coat, the pockets of which were habitually stuffed with pipe, tobacco and matches. He liked this place, deeply, despite the human hellfire his sophisticated machines kept track of and tried to control.

It was one of the most complex computer centers known to man.

Stony Man's computer room harbored three futuristic machines, including the compact but still powerful IBM System 370-158, which with its main computer storage capacity of one to two million characters was the most frequently used in backing up Mack Bolan's terrorist wars.

The system included such recent breakthroughs as bubble memory, composed of small magnetic domains formed on a thin crystal film of synthetic garnet; high-resolution graphic output devices that could display complex images in several different colors on CRT screens for maps, bar charts, graphic creations of all kinds; ''light pens'' that could write directly onto the screens to enter or alter data. Stony Man spared no expense to acquire the latest peripherals.

The system, under Kurtzman's control, would soon be able to process an incredible eighty million instructions per second. Already it was linked to the Intelsat system, whose satellites provided six hundred twenty-five pathways with which to beam information around the world.

The ''artificial intelligence'' of Stony Man's computer room was in fact the most potent weapon in Mack Bolan's considerable arsenal, although armorer Andrjez Konzaki would spunkily dispute such an idea. It cost a fortune, courtesy of the American people, but what it was saving in lives and institutions made it the only truly sound investment the nation had taken for the safety of each and every tomorrow.

As Kurtzman lit his pipe—and the nearby ecologizer inhaled the impurities from the air—a laser printer spewed out information that the Bear had "fetched." The machine's quiet humming underscored Kurtzman's excitement, like a kid with a new toy. This printer could sprint. It fired out in excess of twenty thousand lines per minute. Kurtzman smiled openly as the machine belted out the information; man's technology had surely taken a giant step beyond man.

His thoughts were interrupted by the gentle closing of a door. He turned to greet April Rose. She was the person who kept the huge hi-tech intelligence center in the Shenandoah Mountains running as crisply and as accurately as a Swiss watch. She was the heart—just as Mack Bolan was the soul—of Stony Man Farm.

"For you," she said as she sidled up to Kurtzman and handed him a cup of coffee. "I'm glad you've got your nose away from a screen. You'll go blind staring at those things fifteen hours a day."

The coffee he sipped, the advise he canned—Aaron Kurtzman belonged in front of the Stony Man CRTs, and there was nowhere else he wanted to be.

"I'm getting what we need for DiAlto," he told her. "This thing's burping it out like a well-fed baby," he added as new data scrolled up on the screen.

"You're slowing down," April said. "Your search took almost four minutes."

Kurtzman smiled benignly. "I'll have it transmitted directly to the system in Italy. Won't take a second."

"Good," April said as she walked to the door. "Mack's on his way to Bellagio. When DiAlto gets your information on Savasta, he'll get it to Mack. I hate being out of touch with Striker, but it's the only way to go on this. At least we have Colonel DiAlto as liaison."

"He sounds a sterling character," answered Kurtzman. "Poor bastard."

April walked down a long, permanently lighted passageway toward Hal Brognola's quarters. She made a striking figure as she strode down the empty corridor, her bearing purposeful and strong, her hair catching the light, reflecting rich shades of reddish brown. She was tall and confident and achingly lonely.

Ever since the personal assault on Mack Bolan's life by a KBG operative known as Vigoury, she had been consumed by anxiety about further campaigns by other shadow men. A terrorist net had a pattern profile on Colonel John Phoenix, and that fact had put April Rose on the defensive.

But whenever she felt a fresh wave of concern threaten to overwhelm her, she braced herself with the knowledge that Stony Man's data net had a far wider catch range than anything even the KBG or GRU had in current operation.

If the ''get-Phoenix'' domino theory really was in action, whereby a successful hit against Vigoury's gang only cleared the way for a strike from another team, then the Bear's mammoth computer operation, with its logic operations and function-speed in nano-seconds, would unfailingly anticipate the sequence of moves and rush to assist Stony Man's hardpunching avengers in their search to destroy.

Now the field of action had shifted to Italy, to the olive-colored hills of a Mediterranean country far removed from the green Appalachian range that held the mountains of Stony Man and Hawks Bill. The task at hand was different too. No longer was the security of John Phoenix, or Stony Man Farm, uppermost on Mack Bolan's mind; his concern now was to counter the tragic failure of NATO security overseas.

NATO commanders in Europe had long since concluded that their personnel, let alone nuclear missile sites, were open targets for terrorists. Security had been particularly lax in previous decades, because little had been invested in it during the cash-short period of the Vietnam War. In 1972, in fact, as Hal had once told April with outrage in his voice, a U.S. investigator had arrived at an American post in West Germany and found unlocked and unguarded the door to the basement of a building where nuclear weapons were stored.

Security improvements had been slowed for years by the endless wrangling between combined bureaucracies of the Pentagon, NATO headquarters and the ministries of defense, interior and commerce of NATO member nations.

The U.S. Defense Department had recently, and at last, upgraded its Long Range Security Program in Europe, but the program relied largely on band-aid improvements such as increased patrols, gas masks, flak jackets, sandbags.... It was evidently not enough.

Sometimes, April concluded ruefully as she reached Hal's door, it takes a bloody attack like Vigoury's to wake people up. Maybe the Red Justice Column was doing the bureaucracies that favor right now.

"Hal?" she questioned, as she quietly opened the door. The White House liaison jumped in his chair, his teeth chomping through the unlit stogie parked between his teeth.

"Hellfire," Hal Brognola complained. "You gotta

make more noise when you come in or you'll give me a heart attack." The two pieces of cigar were unceremoniously chucked into the wastebasket.

"Glad you're here anyway. Just got a call from our friend in New York," he reported, cooling down. "He's got some information and he's insistent he fly to Italy to deliver it to Striker personally. And to give Striker a hand, of course. You know our friend's appetite for action."

"What do you think?" asked April. "Should he go?"

"One way or another, Striker needs the information, and I've got a hunch he'd be kinda happy to see our buddy in the front lines again."

If April Rose had her way, Mack Bolan would have help on every mission—and it would come in the form of a long-legged young woman who answered to the name of April Rose.

"I say we do it," she said. "Let's send him."

"Settled. Our friend will be in Italy just as soon as we get him there."

"Hal, tell me one more time," April said softly, the concern visible in her darkening eyes as the lush curls of her hair fell about her high cheekbones. "Why do we put Mack into the heart of the death zones all the time?"

"You know as well as I do." Hal smiled, reaching forward from his chair to hold April's hand. "We do it because life without action is a failure for Mack.

And the action today is counterterrorism. That's the way it is. Remember, Mack Bolan can no more help being a complete man than you can help being a very beautiful woman.''

April Rose returned the smile, with gratitude. "He is a complete man, isn't he?''

"He has the most advanced fighting mind of anyone in recent history,'' Hal confirmed. "That much we know for sure. Every mission proves it. Even his vacations prove it. And I try to get into that mind. I read his reports, sometimes he lets me see his journal. I am in awe of what I find there. Sometimes I join him mentally in battle, and I'm stunned time and time again by his intuitive skill at striking first, and fast. It all begins in his mind. But how he translates it into action is beyond me.''

"Only historians will have the last word on that,'' said April. "They'll look at Mack in the future and they'll have a field day.''

She turned to leave. She had to return to Kurtzman and his consoles to take continuing action in the war to preserve freedom.

For history was being made this very day.

4

WHAP.

The sentry dropped to the ground in a heap, not making a sound, not knowing what hit him. Blood spilled from a large gash on the back of his head caused by the deadly butt of an AutoMag. Mack Bolan's AutoMag.

Having disposed of the sentry, Bolan crouched low in the lifeless gloom at the base of an olive tree. A master cracker of defenses, Bolan was on the offensive once again, attempting to penetrate, seek and save.

The Executioner was rigged hard for the hit. He was rigged to the hilt.

The Beretta 93-R was back in its elongated leather holster. Over the years, one Beretta or another had become almost a part of Bolan, an extension of his firing arm.

The stainless steel AutoMag, Big Thunder, was back on his right hip after being bounced off the skull of the guard. He carried extra clips for both weapons on a combat harness, along with strangulation gear, grenades, plastique, a Fairbairon-Sykes knife.

Bolan had donned his blacksuit. A black cosmetic, smeared on his face, completed the nighttime effect. The Executioner was just another shadow in the pre-dawn light.

He wore a Nitefinder TH-70 eye shield. The Nitefinder, which operates by infrared, intensifies light until pitch darkness turns into dusk.

Bolan scanned the enemy turf from the top of a small hill, looking closely for traces of people who might be waiting for intruders like the Executioner.

It had been a short journey from Como. During the drive, Bolan was contacted by Mike DiAlto via the compact transceiver the big guy wore on his belt. The compact unit linked Bolan to DiAlto and company via a NATO scrambler station, which gave the transmissions airtight security and added range.

From his post in Milan, Colonel DiAlto had traced the names through the Stony Man computers the other side of the Atlantic. *Savasta*, DiAlto had said, translated into Gaspare Cesare Savasta, a senator in the *Partito Communisti Italiano* (PCI), one of Italy's six major political parties. Savasta, DiAlto revealed, had a summer home on the outskirts of Bellagio.

Bolan continued to survey the undulating terrain of Savasta's estate. Through the glow of the goggles, he saw no sign of movement. All was still in the silence of the early morning.

The big guy considered the area he was dealing with. He went over the surrounding terrain, drawing maps in his mind, storing them for future reference.

Bellagio is set amid soaring peaks and lush Mediterranean vegetation. Lake Como straddles the retreat to the north.

Bolan knew the sleepy little village had more private villas than it had public accommodations. He thought it a strange place for a terrorist hideout.

At first glance, the Communist senator's estate looked like any of a number of similar properties that Bolan's rented Maserati had passed along the outskirts of the town. Surrounding these estates were formidable brick walls, about ten feet high. This was millionaire country. The wealthy enjoyed their privacy and security.

The Savasta estate's guise of respectability was quickly shot to hell by a close inspection of the place.

The main entrance to the grounds was set in the northwest corner of the wall. The entrance, designed to discourage gate-crashing, angled in such a way that no vehicle could pick up enough speed to ram through the reinforced fence. A brick guardhouse stood tall behind the iron gate, and Bolan clearly discerned two sentries toting what he guessed to be VB Bernardelli submachine guns.

Very professional.

Beyond the gate and the guardhouse, the estate extended in a rolling, ever-gradual incline toward a massive house, about eighteen hundred yards up a pebblestone drive.

Bolan made his way toward the outer wall. He saw no more guards in the immediate area—the sentry he had hit was a lone scout who had been patrolling outside the confines of the estate with a telltale sweep of his submachine gun. Bolan had recognized the type immediately—mean and dull-faced, illegally armed, working at night in a zone earmarked by Intelligence· a terrorist.

It was a moonless night. The Executioner negotiated the wall with extreme caution. Taking a short run at the structure, he leaped and planted his right foot on the wall, then used the foot as a springboard, powering himself up so that he could reach and grab the top. With a hand over the tiles that formed a peak along the wall, he lifted himself up and over, and unloaded himself onto the other side.

He did a quick scan of the area, making sure that none of the guards had heard his light thump as he landed on the enemy side.

The coast was clear.

The big guy crept toward the main house, keeping to the inky shadows of shrubbery and clusters of trees that dotted the landscape. Whenever possible Bolan hugged those shadows. He knew that Savasta's security men would be equipped with night-vision devices.

The longer he could avoid a clash with the guards the better.

First flickers of dawn were inching over the eastern horizon. The last minutes before dawn broke would find the guards sleepy, bored after hours of night-watching, eager for their replacements to arrive. The sentries would be off guard. They would be careless.

The Executioner moved on a course roughly parallel to the long, curved gravel driveway. When he reached the edge of a tree line, twenty yards from the clearing that surrounded the main house and another building, he stopped for further recon.

Senator Savasta's summer retreat was a beautiful villa—modern, expansive and luxurious. The house was shaped like a huge U, with the main entrance located front center in the bottom portion of the U. A courtyard, dominated by a large fountain, stood in front of the main entrance.

Two sentries were posted near the fountain, cradling Russian-manufactured AK-47 automatic rifles across their cocked left arms. The men were young, barely into their twenties, clothed in casual sweaters and slacks. But there was nothing casual in the way they scanned the grounds like eagles looking for prey. The battlewise Bolan stayed united with the shadows.

About twenty yards from the main building stood a modern one-story structure that no doubt served as a barracks for the security staff.

And that was the scene, the battleground, that Bolan saw spread before him. Somewhere, presumably in one of the two buildings, Louise and Angel DiAlto were being held hostage.

The secluded villa of a sympathetic left-wing senator had been turned into a "people's prison."

The man in black sucked in a big breath of early morning air, palmed the silenced Beretta and left the tree line.

5

As Bolan closed in on the barracks, he reached into a pouch on the combat harness and grabbed a clump of plastique.

The sun was rising. He had to move fast.

In the barracks of Villa Savasta, early-morning sounds could be heard as life returned. Groggy voices, still blanketed with sleep, carried across the morning stillness.

Bolan knew the voices must be dealt with before they had a chance to shake the grogginess from their tone.

Keeping a distance so that he would not be spotted by the two guards at the front entrance, the black-suited warrior circled the barracks. He was trying to gain information on the setup, trying to gain an edge.

The hostages would be stashed in the main house, if they were at the Villa Savasta at all. The barracks were not large enough to house both prisoners and security staff.

Bolan planted himself behind a corner of the low barracks building.

Peering around the corner, he saw a guard answering a pressing call of nature with a quick piss on one of the senator's shrubs.

As Bolan moved into view, the guard's eyes widened in alarm. The guard shouted at another guy coming through the back doorway of the barracks, but his sentence was stopped as Bolan triggered a pencil of saffron flame from the Beretta. The sentry's face exploded as a 9mm bullet bore into skull, leaving nothing but spurting blood and a dead man in its wake.

The second guard never made it through the doorway. The Beretta tracked on cue. Another flame slashed the dawn's dim light. The hardguy, blood spilling out of a hole in his skull, stumbled back into the building.

Only seconds had passed since the Executioner had turned that corner and dealt out death. But in those passing seconds, the hit had gone intentionally hard. Inside the security barracks there was the sound of mad scurrying, the sound of people trying to get organized.

Bolan would not let them get organized. He would not give them the luxury of time. No time for the plastic explosive; he tugged a grenade from his belt.

The Beretta scanning for danger. Bolan yanked out the pin from the grenade with his teeth. He tossed the grenade, fused for five seconds, into the back doorway.

The Executioner was well past the door when the explosion erupted, fire balling out parts of bodies and brickwork. The thunderclap was horribly magnified in the enclosed space. The ground shivered under Bolan's feet.

Shouts and cries came from inside the building, some startled, some suffering.

Bolan unwrapped the clump of plastique and stooped to plant the powerful HE at the base of a hedge. The hedge ran alongside the building. A perfect place for a little fireworks. He inserted a triggered time fuse, then continued on.

He legged it around another corner and made fast tracks toward a door, twenty yards across a stretch of sloping lawn. The door was one of many entrances into the ground floor of Gaspare Savasta's villa.

Lights showed in more and more windows as the occupants of the main house reacted to the noise.

An aggravated voice from inside the villa barked orders in the direction of the guard barracks.

In the final heartbeat before Bolan reached the door, two terrorist commandos appeared before him, probing the area with their AK-47s. Bolan quickfired the Beretta, dropping the pair in their tracks before they had a chance to respond to the chilling sight of the big man in black.

The midnight warrior gained the door. He tried the handle. Quickly he stepped back and launched a kick into the lock. The door slapped open.

Bolan entered the house. He was in the kitchen. Soundlessly he slipped through a pantry, moved into a dining room. He bee-lined toward the front of the house. He could hear footsteps coming from the floor above and footsteps clattering on the basement floor downstairs. He quit the dining room and emerged in the wide recesses of a foyer.

The front doorway was filled by a guard gripping a Czech Scorpion machine pistol in one hand and the doorknob in the other. He was looking out across the grounds in the direction of the guard barracks. The man suddenly sensed the presence of an intruder. He started to turn, tracking the machine pistol.

At the same instant, from the corner of his eye, Bolan saw three men tromping down a staircase, one ahead, the other two a step behind. The first terrorist toted a Beretta 92-S. The other two held Ingram M-10s.

Sightings on all sides happened within the blink of an eye.

Someone from the floor above yelled a cry of alarm in a guttural Eastern European tongue.

The scene exploded.

The Beretta in Bolan's hand chugged twice. The guard at the doorway spun on his heels and fell outside, his face blown away.

Bolan shifted the Beretta to his left hand. He filled his right fist with the .44 AutoMag. Big Thunder's bolting report filled the room.

The lead terrorist on the stairway fell in an awkward tumble over the banister. Much of his head was left behind, splattered across the other two guards.

The two remaining terrorists separated to either side of the stairs, both churning bullets down to the warrior at the base of the stairs.

Bolan dived to the marble floor and took aim at the ripping fire from above, sighting both the Beretta and the AutoMag up the stairs as bullets hissed around his head.

The big .44 rode a wild recoil as the Magnum headbuster sprayed skull and brains down the stairs. The silenced Beretta issued slugs that made neat work of drilling through the other hardguy's head.

Four dead guards.

The gunfire stopped. The stench of cordite and ruptured flesh filled the area. Puddles of blood spread across the floor.

More clatter, more commotion came from an arched hallway visible at the top of the stairway.

Footsteps. Shouting.

The Executioner took the stairs three at a time. He reached the top and nearly collided with a pockmarked punk coming around the corner with a Scorpion.

Bolan smashed him with the butt of the AutoMag, forcing the guy's nose into his skull. The man's body somersaulted down the stairs, bones crunching en route.

Bolan bounced a glance down the upper hallway, hitting the floor in the same motion.

Two terrorists, loaded down with side arms and automatic rifles, were stationed at a door midway down the hall. They unslung their AKs, preparing to protect the door and what was housed behind it with their lives.

The AutoMag bucked four times in rapid succession. The sentries were kicked backward to the floor.

Bolan ran to the door the sentries had been guarding.

He was acutely aware of the buzz of activity that was drifting up from the lower level and from outside. The air was alive with men shouting.

Reaching the door, Bolan exploded with a kick that stripped the wood from the hinges.

6

BOLAN HAD BUSTED INTO A BEDROOM. A fantasy bedroom. A weird playpen for sexual sadism.

The big guy did a double-take.

The room was littered with the tools of sadism. The decor was dressed up with the trimmings of a fairy tale—complete with sky blue walls and a magnificent canopy bed—and then defaced with chains, torture devices, and a long whip that sat like a coiled python on the white shag carpet that covered the floor.

From a corner of the room, the Executioner heard a muffled moan. He moved to a curtain that cut off the corner from the rest of the room. Behind it, strung up from the ceiling, was a woman.

The woman's hands, extended high above her head, were bound by a skipping rope, which, in turn, was tied to a large hook in the ceiling.

Stripped to the waist, the woman's breasts were bruised, the targets of a brutal hand. Her back, raw and blistered, had been savagely stroked by the whip.

Hanging from the rope, her mouth covered with

tape, the woman twisted and turned in a mad panic, not knowing if Bolan had come as a savage or a savior.

"Easy," he said, mixing comfort and authority in his voice even as rage boiled his blood.

Like lightning, he swung the AutoMag, triggering a round toward the door, blowing away two overly curious guards who had raced into the bedroom. The guards dropped, their blood spilling out onto the white rug.

Bolan took another quick survey of the room before returning his attention to the suspended woman.

Grabbing his knife, the big guy cut the rope with one quick slash. The woman dropped to the floor. Bolan caught her, righted her and peeled the tape from her mouth.

She was not Louise DiAlto.

Bolan brought to mind the snapshots he had studied of Louise DiAlto. Louise was blond, almost five foot ten and of very compact build.

The woman with Bolan was about twenty-six, twenty-seven, about five foot seven, with a beautiful build, dark shoulder-length hair and flashing dark eyes. Her skin, save for where she had been abused, was golden.

The woman searched the room and found her ripped blouse. She walked over to one of the dead guards, picked up an Ingram and gripped it with an assurance that impressed the man in black.

"Do you speak English?" he asked in a low whisper.

"Yes," she said.

"Colonel John Phoenix," Bolan said. They stood to the left of the open door, their backs to the wall.

"Gia. Gia Vallone," she answered, smiling for a moment, gripping his arm with warmth and thankfulness.

Bolan motioned her to keep quiet. Gia, also hearing feet padding up the stairs, stood in silence beside him.

Both were ready to blow away anything that entered the room. But evidently no one dared. The footsteps stopped just outside the room. Chicken shits.

Bolan wondered if Gia would be able to help him. She looked shaken up, but she also looked a thoroughbred.

"You okay?" he whispered, his voice barely audible.

She did not answer, just nodded. That was all the nightscorcher needed. He knew that in a crunch—and the crunch was now—he could count on this woman.

Before taking on the guards, he wanted information.

"Louise DiAlto," Bolan said. "Is she here?"

"No," Gia said. "I was trying to get word out."

"Is there any other way out of here besides those stairs?"

"Down the hall, then to the left. Servants' stairs behind the door."

"Let's do it then, Gia," he grunted. He dived across the open door.

Big Thunder blazed their path to freedom. Both of the chicken guards in the hall, aiming their machine pistols at chest level, paid the ultimate price for their temerity. Bolan sailed slightly under their sights, firing from floor level.

The two Ingrams opened fire at the first sign of movement, but their chatter merely stitched the walls and decorations.

Big Thunder put the gun talk to rest in microseconds, before the guards could adjust their high line of fire. The two thugs died.

More guards were swarming to the area.

Gia had followed Bolan into the hallway, trailing the big guy by a few steps. With apparent lack of concern for her own welfare, she crouched, tagging the terrorists with fire from the Ingram.

The air was filled with spraying shots of blood. Bodies were strewn on the floor.

The terrorists had been stifled. For now.

Bolan fed the hungry AutoMag another clip. With Gia hot on his tail, the two ran to the servants' stairs.

Gia, knowing the terrain, led the way down the

twisting stairs. "I've got a car waiting outside the wall," Bolan said.

Without breaking stride the woman answered: "We'll never make it that far on foot. The garage is below. Follow me. I have a car there."

They reached the stairwell leading into the basement garage. They entered the garage. The parking area was large enough to accommodate a dozen or more cars, but it was only half full.

Two sentries, their butts parked on the bumper of a Mercedes, spotted the intruders and jumped into action.

Bolan and his partner separated, gunning into battle like well-oiled, fine-tuned machines.

Bolan caught the guy on the right with a .44 round that turned the guy's throat into torn strands of flesh. Gushing blood spilled onto the Mercedes, spoiling its polished shine.

The Ingram in Gia's hands fired one round, carrying enough power to punch the other sentry backward across the hood of the car and onto the garage floor.

The sounds of the gunfire echoed wildly in the cavernous garage.

Gia pointed to an Alfa Romeo.

"It's mine," she stated. "The keys are in it."

The pair dashed to the car, Gia giving way to Bolan, letting him get behind the wheel. He gunned the engine. Tires ignited in a burned-rubber protest as he spun in a tight circle and floored the gas pedal, upshifting as the sporty machine bolted up an incline out of the garage.

Daylight collided with the windshield. A guard collided with the front fender. The car lifted the man and tossed him over the hood, his body as flexible as a rag doll.

Bolan kept the pedal kissing the floor.

Suddenly the earth shivered from the blast that engulfed the security barracks. The timer fuse in the planted plastique had brought the explosive to life.

A fireball blossomed as the car roared by. Flames reached up and licked the sky, choking smoke engulfed the area. Wood, mortar, bits and pieces of bodies showered the Alfa Romeo.

"American fireworks?" Gia said, shielding her eyes from the blast.

Terrorists—those who weren't eaten by the blast—aimed at the speeding car. Their shots missed as Bolan masterfully zigzagged the surging machine.

His mind leaped ahead to an upcoming problem. The gate with its angled design was crash proof. The nightfighter hoped a grenade would turn the trick.

Piloting the sports car down the winding driveway, he tugged the grenade from his belt.

It would take some fancy wheelwork, but there was a chance that he and Gia might be able to swerve in on the guards at the gate, pitch the grenade and bust out of the smoldering hellgrounds.

He accelerated the car like a racing driver through the last sharp bend in the driveway.

Negotiating the turn, Bolan saw a panel truck strategically parked across the drive just ahead of him.

Bolan slammed the car's brake pedal to the floor, knowing the move was probably too late.

Beside him Gia Vallone screamed.

7

MACK BOLAN HAD ONLY a few short heartbeats of time in which to react. Those blurred moments were framed by Gia's scream and the shrill squeal of the Alfa Romeo's tires.

"Bail out!" he yelled.

As the car sailed on toward the panel truck, Bolan tumbled out in a calculated spill. Sighting the car as he dropped, he saw the falling frame of Gia Vallone.

Bolan did not know much about this woman, but he knew she had guts.

Bolan hit the lush carpet of lawn only feet shy of the impact. Landing with the practiced agility of a stuntman, he rolled once, twice, three times, away from the crash that was rocking the silence with the smash of colliding metal.

He quickly recovered from the rolls, coming back up on his feet. With a sideways glance, he saw Gia steadying herself after breaking her fall with the same roll technique. Despite the shock and the bruising, both came up tracking with weapons of death.

The Alfa Romeo and the truck had met in a grinding climax of destruction. The sound was piercing. From behind the panel truck, running like scared rats in hell, three terrorists leaped to safety.

One of them toted a pump shotgun. The other two were outfitted with AKs.

Bolan took out the guy with the shotgun, using the AutoMag to peg him in the head with a .44 caliber punch. The guy's cranium exploded in a halo of blood and brain matter.

Another terrorist was sent crashing to the ground, his face peppered by the dead-eye aim of Gia Vallone.

Only one creep remained. The guy had already closed his finger on his AK's trigger when three slugs fired from Gia's Ingram in three-shot mode landed solidly in his heart. The slugs erupted. Bloody bits of flesh and bone burst out of a gaping hole in the guy's back. The man spun like a top, the AK-47 firing off a short burst into the air before it fell from dead fingers.

The scene settled. Surrounding noises rang with clarity.

Shouts closed in from front and rear.

The big American and the gutsy Italian beauty cut across the manicured estate grounds, shielded by clusters of shrubs.

Bolan's power-packed legs carried his full frame at great speed; Gia, her strides shorter but quicker, kept up with him.

Bolan looked over his shoulder as a light truck came whipping around the bend in the driveway behind them.

"My car's just over that wall," Bolan called to Gia. "But we need breathing room. You take the bastards from the gate, I'll take the truck...."

The warrior in black—an easy sight now that dawn had broken through the blanket of night—sped away from the woman.

A shot rang out from the direction of the terrorists approaching on foot. Gia's Ingram rattled, driving back the three guards, providing good cover for Bolan.

The pickup truck two-wheeled it around the curve of the pebbled driveway. Two men rode in the cab, three more hung on for their lives in the backbed. All were armed with heavy automatic weapons: Uzis and AKs.

The driver targeted the two figures with his eyes, tugged the steering wheel, sent the vehicle up onto the grass, an unstoppable machine speeding toward Mack Bolan.

The rapid, rampant report of Gia's Ingram, along with answering fire from downrange, was steady in the Executioner's ears.

Big Thunder spit. It scored a direct hit that burst the tire just as the pickup's wheel dropped into an eroded dip in the terrain.

It was too much for the driver to handle. It was too

much for *any* driver to handle. The pickup cart-wheeled nose over tail. Bodies, arms and legs wind-milling, were tossed into the air.

One of the hardguys was pitched ahead of the truck and the vehicle landed on him. The guy's body was crushed like a fly.

The pickup was upside down, its wheels spinning madly in the air. The engine sputtered and died. So did the driver, his head banged and lacerated to bits by the windshield.

The passenger crawled out of the overturned cab and scrambled to escape his date with fate. A .44 whizzer clipped away about one-third of his head and sent the rest nose diving into the ground.

The two remaining terrorists, flung from the flying vehicle, had taken cover behind the truck. They carried AK-47s and a large grudge against the Executioner.

Mack Bolan pumped off two rounds, hesitating only seconds between shots to accommodate the hand cannon's bucking-bronco recoil. The two rounds kept the enemy down.

In the distance Bolan could see at least half a dozen men closing in from high ground. He glanced over at Gia Vallone. She had sent two terrorists to their graves while the third guard took refuge behind a pine tree. The guy leaned around the tree and fired a wild shot. Gia saw him. She squeezed the trigger of her Ingram. It was silent. Empty.

Bolan swung Big Thunder around in a straight-armed arc. He sighted over Gia's shoulder. The woman was defenseless; his shot had to be target perfect. Flame lanced out of the Magnum muzzle. The targeted figure flung his arms out as he was pitched backward. Within seconds he was dead. Gia ran to the man and seized his Uzi.

"We can make it to the wall," Bolan said. "We've got to move fast."

As the word "fast" left his lips, he tossed two more rounds to keep the enemy pinned behind the overturned truck. Then they were off, sprinting for their lives.

Moments before they reached the wall, more gunfire rang out. Bolan did not pause to return the fire: the odds spoke too highly in favor of the opposition. The route to survival was the wall. The bottom line was to get himself and Gia the hell over the wall.

He gave the long driveway an over-the-shoulder glance. Two more vehicles, packed with terrorists, were tearing down the road in a mad race to intercept Bolan and Gia.

Slugs whistled through the air, pinging into the yellow stucco wall, as Bolan and Gia reached its base.

The Executioner lifted himself to the top of the wall, using the same fluid motion he had employed the first time.

The Executioner saw what he wanted to see. Partially concealed in a grove of olive trees on the other side of the wall sat his Maserati, at this moment his freedom machine.

He triggered some hot rounds to slow down the advancing foot troops. Then he crouched and extended his left arm, offering his hand to Gia. She leaped, reached the arm and he started to pull her up.

Bolan felt a sudden cold-hot stinging sensation as a bullet whizzed a mere fraction of an inch past his right ear.

Gia, struggling slightly, reached the top of the wall. The pair stood ready to leap toward freedom.

Another wild storm of gunfire clouded the area.

Gia whirled around with violent force. She would have toppled headfirst off the wall except that Bolan grabbed her, and balanced himself and her on the red-tile top.

She was limp in his arms.

Gia Vallone had stopped a bullet.

8

BOLAN, GRABBING HER UZI before it fell to the ground, saw a hole in Gia Vallone's blouse. The rip was quickly framed by blood. Her eyes flickered with the shock that had buckled her knees. She grasped her left shoulder and gasped for breath. She looked up at Bolan, her eyes quickly clearing.

"I'm okay," she said.

"Then move," he said softly, "and keep low."

She gave Bolan a final glance, then dropped to the ground. Suddenly a car was hurtling toward her.

Gia raced across the road and reached the Maserati just as the accelerating car gunned by. Machine-gun muzzles poked out of the windows and fired. Gia dived face-first behind the Maserati.

By the time the car roared past him, Bolan had yanked a grenade from his side and hurled the primed explosive through the driver's open window. "Bull's-eye," he grunted.

A thunderclap sounded from within the car, followed closely by an eruption of flame. All screams ceased abruptly in the confined space as glass, metal and bodies were violently mixed.

Bolan, who had stretched out flat atop the wall, lifted his head as soon as the blast was complete. The car was smoldering junk. Bolan could see nothing of the terrorists except small portions of their mutilated bodies.

The Executioner put Gia's Uzi into action and sketched a round at the advancing "liberation fighters" from his perch atop the wall. Bullets ripped at his feet. He dropped to the ground and ran over to where he had last seen Gia, diving into the dirt.

The woman was getting to her feet, still behind the cover provided by the Maserati. Seeing Bolan, not seeing any terrorists, she straightened up and hurried toward the passenger side of the car.

Some of the bullets fired at Gia had hit the Maserati. The car had sustained about half a dozen small holes. Bolan sat in the driver's seat and turned the ignition switch. The car came through, purring to life.

Bolan drove out of the small grove of trees, pointing the car away from Bellagio. He was just in time to see a second terrorist pursuit car bolting out of the villa grounds in a killing quest.

Bolan knew the Maserati could outrun the tailing car. But he also knew that such a race might take the two cars to a populated area—an area where innocent people could get caught in the firefight.

In front of him stretched flat terrain. The road

was bordered on either side by meadow. It was the kind of area he could use to his advantage.

He eased up on the gas pedal, keeping a close vigil on the hardguys in the tailing car. He allowed the other vehicle to gain.

"Can you steer with your good arm?" he asked Gia.

"I'll try," she answered, reaching for the wheel with her right hand.

"Don't steer in a straight line," he instructed. "Make us a tough target."

Bolan pushed the accelerator and, at the same moment, Gia began yanking the wheel. Back and forth the car wheeled, picking up speed.

The tail car continued its chase. Bullets bounced off the Maserati's chassis.

Bolan, his foot still on the gas pedal, carefully turned his upper body and leaned out of the window. He took aim, then squeezed off a round from the AutoMag.

The tail car's windshield crumbled. The driver slumped lifelessly over the wheel, turning the vehicle into an uncontrollable swerve. Veering off the road, hiking itself up on two wheels, the car continued on in two-wheel helldriver form until it was finally flipped by gravity. It landed on its roof.

The Executioner did not turn back to dispose of the terrorists who survived the crash. At least they were out of his hair and, with time racing toward death for Louise and Angel DiAlto, proceeding with the mission was priority one.

Bolan sent the Maserati headed south at the first crossroads they encountered.

Gia Vallone leaned back, happy her stint as a stunt driver had come to a successful end, pleased her brush with terrorist scum was behind her. She let out a large sigh. Closing her eyes—as if by closing her eyes she could shut out the pain and increasing numbness in her shoulder—she let her lips form a small smile. She was thankful to be alive.

Brushing her hair from her face, she finally opened her eyes and looked at the large man piloting the car.

"We have lost them, they are gone," she said. "Signor Phoenix, you are *magnifico*. Thank you for coming to my rescue."

Bolan accepted her thanks with a nod. He glanced at her shoulder.

"How's your wound?"

"I will live. It's as if a bee stung me," she said, understating the pain. "Well, perhaps a dozen bees. I am very lucky. We're both very lucky."

"Who are you, Gia? NOCS?"

"With your weapons you are deadly, the deadliest I've ever seen. With your mind you are sharp. NOCS is correct," she said, her brown eyes sparkling.

"Back there," Bolan said, "what happened? How was your cover blown?"

"I infiltrated the Red Justice Column four months

ago," she explained. "Last night I was among those scheduled to transport Signora DiAlto and the child to a new location, a new 'people's prison' as they call them."

"Do you know where it is?"

"No. Upon our arrival at Villa Savasta, I was taken by force to the room where you found me. We, myself and four others, had been loaned from the Milano Column to help escort the DiAltos. Those who were chosen and traveled with me to Bellagio did not suspect that I was an infiltrator. They were as surprised as I was at what happened to me when we arrived."

"Didn't you hear anything, anything at all that could help us, Gia?"

"On our way to Bellagio, the city of Florence was mentioned. I know nothing more. I have no idea what happened to the DiAltos."

The more distance Bolan logged between them and the hellground at Villa Savasta, the more he eased their speed. He reached for the transceiver at his belt.

"Who's your NOCS superior?" he asked Gia.

Ingrained security precautions forced Gia to pause for a moment. Her soulful Italian eyes studied Bolan unblinkingly as her mind raced over the factors. If it had not been for the superb warrior, she would have still been tied up waiting for death. She decided to give.

"Signor Vianake is my control officer. Do you know of him?"

"Yeah, I know him," nodded Bolan. "He's one of my contacts."

He lifted the compact transceiver and depressed the unit's transmit button. "This is Striker to Mother Hen. Come in, Mother Hen."

The transistorized crackle of Colonel DiAlto's voice promptly responded.

"This is Mother Hen. Go ahead, Striker. Uh, do you have the package?"

The package he so casually, almost calmly inquired about was his wife and his young daughter. Bolan hated like hell to have to deliver the news.

"Negative. Sorry. Are you alone?"

"At the moment," DiAlto replied. "Vianake was called away about thirty minutes ago."

"That figures," growled Bolan.

Bolan's sliced statement sparked a pause at the other end as DiAlto considered the American warrior's words and absorbed the disappointment of the news he had just heard.

Bolan knew that DiAlto had insisted on being allowed to have a hand in this operation. DiAlto knew of John Phoenix's involvement and was using the Executioner's combat code name. In some ways, Bolan thought, DiAlto was just too damned close to the situation: this could cause complications. But Bolan himself would have insisted on the same thing had he been in DiAlto's position.

DiAlto's voice again cracked through the static.

He did a good job of keeping in check his emotions.

"About Vianake.... Ah, do I read you correctly, Striker?"

"I think you do," Bolan replied. "But I can't be sure about it. Not yet, anyway. I need you to do some legwork before I get there."

"Name it, Striker. What do you require?"

"Just a needle in a haystack. The Tuscany region around Florence is the only lead we've got at this point. Research this Senator Savasta some more. Dig deep. I've got a hunch he's the key to this thing."

"Okay, I'm on it. Anything else?"

"That's it, Mike. Tread softly. Don't trust anyone. I'll be arriving at your headquarters soon."

"Business as usual, right. Got it. Over and out, Striker."

The connection was broken. Bolan clipped the transceiver to his belt.

The Executioner and the NOCS agent traveled toward Milan in a wide southwestern arc away from Bellagio. Driving on secondary roads that cut through the countryside, they avoided the congestion of traffic.

The morning sun, a fiery ball in the sky, blazed down on the pair. The sun heated the car with a comforting warmth, but in the Maserati, the atmosphere was growing cool, ridden with tension.

Bolan was aware that Gia Vallone was studying him in a new light. His own eyes were busy between the rearview mirror and the stretch of highway that lay ahead.

Traffic in the agricultural region was moderate: trucks on their way to market; the odd cart, pulled by a donkey or horse. But no vehicles pursued them. Bolan had given them the slip.

After miles of silence, Gia told Bolan: "You are mistaken. Captain Vianake has been with the NOCS for years. Since before I joined."

"Captain Vianake is an unknown factor," he countered. "And so are you."

The temperature in the car dropped several more degrees. Cool falling to cold.

"Even after Bellagio?" she asked. "Forgive me, *signor*. I do not understand. What does it take to earn your trust?"

"Gut feeling," he grunted. "I don't quite have that yet. I don't quite have the whole picture. But that is going to change, damn fast."

9

THE PALACE WAS LOCATED in the hills, thirty kilometers northeast of Florence.

It was a monstrous structure, too much for the eye to handle in a single glance. The grandeur, the aging stateliness of the building could only be described as awesome.

In a room within, a man named Libera was being stripped of every ounce of dignity he had ever possessed.

The ceiling of the room had been knocked out centuries earlier to make a two-level library. The library was trimmed with a balcony, plush carpet, a skylight, a fireplace, and wall upon wall of valuable books. Libera, however, was not there because of any thirst for literature. The thug was being drilled.

Antonio Martella stood in front of Libera, who was seated in a wooden chair in the center of the room. Libera, a top-level crew chief in the Red Justice Column's Ilario Folini group, Bergamo Division, deeply resented Martella.

"I should not be held responsible for what happened this morning,'' Libera shouted, trying to defend himself. "It was one man, and he wasn't human." Libera was defensive. Intimidated. Not the usual state for a man who had supervised three hits this year alone.

A film of sweat glistened across his forehead. His voice quavered, cracked. "I chartered a helicopter as soon as I could to report what happened in Bellagio."

A woman, who until this time had been standing in the corner of the room looking bored with the proceedings, crossed toward him.

"You came here to report?" she spat. "Bullshit. You came here to save your own worthless ass." Her voice was harsh, like an icy cold wind. She swung her steele gaze to Antonio. "This man is a disgrace to our cause."

Antonio met her stare. The woman's eyes finally fell to the floor.

Martella's forehead housed visible effects of strain. "Emilia," he said, addressing the woman. "You are getting out of control."

She was about to reply but he cut her short, moving back in front of Libera.

Martella was through playing games. He lashed out with the back of his hand. Libera caught the blow, full force to the face. The power behind the blow lifted him slightly out of the chair.

"How could one man do all that damage?"

snarled Antonio. "You lie like a bastard just to make yourself look less a fool, a candy-ass fool."

He held back the temptation to strike Libera again. He did not want to make a bad impression on one other person in the room; he must interrogate in the proper manner.

The fourth person in the library was Viktor Karpov. The Russian stood in a corner of the room, watching the scene. Karpov had the heartless eyes of a snake and a pinched, narrow face that registered no emotion.

Karpov was the kingpin in the scene; everyone in the room knew that he was the man with the power. Unlike Libera, Emilia Salerno and Martella—who all wore the Red Column "uniform" of black slacks, sweater and jacket—he was dressed in a dark suit. His look, his manner, his dress—he might as well have stitched a tag on his suitcoat: KGB.

Libera had recovered from the blow to the head.

"The liberation fighters assigned to me at Bellagio were the best we had," insisted Libera. "But they did not stand a chance.... One man. You must believe, Antonio. I—"

His sentence was halted by the hatred and impatience of Emilia. The female terrorist, who wore a Czech Scorpion autopistol strapped low on her right hip, unholstered the weapon and placed the muzzle of the pistol a quarter inch from the base of Libera's skull.

In her mid-twenties, but looking much older, her bony face pockmarked and pasty, she seemed dangerously unglued.

Antonio opened his mouth to protest.

She pulled the trigger. The weapon roared.

A bullet burrowed through Libera's brain, then exploded out above his right eye, spraying blood and bone across the room. The bullet's power kicked the victim from the chair and sent him sprawling facedown on the carpet. A pool of gore began spreading under the body.

Martella, reacting with instinct, touched his own side arm, a German Luger, clipped in cross-draw leather on his belt. He paused and left the weapon at his side when he saw Emilia leathering her Scorpion.

"It is most important that our fighters realize the price they have to pay for failure," she said icily.

Emilia was a true terrorist. Her eyes were those of the walking dead. Everything about her suggested sudden death. She had requested, and had been given, the job of guarding Louise DiAlto and her daughter. Emilia was the heartless bitch who had amputated the hostage's wedding-ring finger. She had not used anesthetic.

Antonio glanced at Karpov. The Russian continued to watch in silence, his eyes missing nothing.

Karpov nodded, almost imperceptibly.

That was enough for Antonio. He had no desire to push a violent confrontation with Emilia at this time.

Not with the powerful Russian looking on. He removed his hand from the butt of the Luger.

"Emilia," he chastised, "you're too goddamn bloodthirsty. Now we will never learn what Libera might have told us about the enemy that launched the attack at Bellagio."

The woman stood unflinching. "Libera was a coward and a fool. There was no single man. Only a highly trained commando unit could have caused such damage."

"And what of Senator Savasta?" Martella insisted. "The old man is close to going over the edge already."

"Then we should assist him, give him a little push over the edge," Emilia snapped. "He is expendable. We are all expendable."

The double doors burst open. Gaspare Savasta stumbled into the library.

The palace where the terrorists had snuffed out Libera's life, the ancient building in which Emilia had just plotted to snuff out Savasta's life, was owned by Gaspare Savasta himself. It was his ancestral home.

The Communist senator, drawn to the library by the pistol shot, gaped at the sight of the dead man sprawled across the carpet.

Savasta, a roly-poly man in his late fifties, was breathing strenuously. The pool of blood was still expanding under Libera's corpse.

"This," he gasped, "this has gone too far." His voice shook as he spoke. He turned to the Russian.

"Karpov, you never said it would be like this. Allowing your forces to billet here is in itself an outrage. I have heard my vacation mansion in Bellagio has been attacked. It's outrageous. I'm ruined. Now *this*."

Karpov, the silent force, did not respond. Instead he turned his back on Savasta and stared contently at a shelf of books.

"Emilia," Antonio commanded, "you will escort our host back to his quarters. Then, see that he is confined there. If he leaves his quarters, shoot him."

"Yes, Antonio," she replied, taking pleasure in the command.

"Also, Emilia, you will see to the removal of Libera—what is left of Libera. Double the guard around Louise DiAlto and the child. I believe we will have to send Colonel DiAlto another reminder soon. The child this time, I think. Wait with them until you hear from me."

Senator Savasta bristled with rage.

"Comrade Karpov, I cannot sanction bloody torture within the walls of my home. I have been lied to and misused."

Emilia grabbed the pudgy man's upper arm and gave him a persuasive shove toward the door.

"Move it, fat boy," she said, disgust in her voice.

"You pledged yourself to our cause. Now you whimper like a child. We are not intellectual players who sit on the sidelines and interpret. The capitalist enemy kills. We kill them, or they kill us."

Emilia spoke as if she were reading slogan placards.

The senator was unceremoniously prodded out of the library. Emilia slammed the door shut behind her as she followed the man out.

Karpov turned from the bookshelves once he and Antonio were alone. Alone with a leaking corpse.

He broke his silence. "She must not kill Savasta," he said.

"Emilia obeys my orders, comrade," Antonio assured.

"Emilia will cause you nothing but trouble. *She* must be killed."

Antonio glanced at the body of Libera. "Sometimes she does not wait for orders. She is too caught up in it all," he said almost wistfully. "There are things that Libera could have told us."

The Russian snorted.

"We know all we need to know. It matters little whether one man or thirty was responsible for the raid on Bellagio. An offensive has been launched against us, that is all we need to know.."

"By the Americans or the Italians?" Antonio wondered aloud. "And the woman, Vallone. Libera said she escaped during the attack."

"I know what Libera said," Karpov growled. "None of it matters. Not the source of this offensive. Not the woman. None of it. All that should concern us is that we can expect to be under attack here in a very short time, by the same force that raided Bellagio. That is our immediate concern. The rest of the puzzle will fall into place."

"There is enough time for us to relocate," Antonio suggested. Immediately he knew he had said the wrong thing to the wrong man.

"Nyet," Karpov barked. "You will note that the various outlets of the media have not reported this morning's action. The Americans and NOCS have contained the incident. This can only mean they plan to continue their attack against us."

"There's still a good chance they won't find us here," Martella said. "Even our contact in the NOCS doesn't know where we moved the hostages after Bellagio."

"They will find us soon enough," Karpov countered. "We are not dealing with blind fools."

"Then why should we remain here? If secrecy is so important...."

"Have you forgotten the other matter, Comrade Martella?" There was a razor-sharp edge to Karpov's voice. "Perhaps the stress of this assignment is too much for you."

Beads of perspiration dotted Antonio's forehead.

"Certainly I remember. But if there is truly a

government informer planted in our ranks—other than that dead fink, Ciucci—what does it matter if he's trapped here or somewhere else?''

"Disappearing in Italy is a child's game," Karpov said in a condescending tone. "We both know that. If we move, the man we want could lose himself, get a new name and a complete new identity and be in another country by this time next week. And he would be free—with our secrets.

"It is essential that we isolate the traitor within our ranks. Immediately. Ciucci has been taken care of. But it goes beyond that punk. The informer is here among us. We must identify and nullify him. If we move and he gets away from us, we will never find him. Also, the men who will identify him for us are due here shortly. Their schedules must be accommodated.''

"If we ourselves cannot move, we should at least move the hostages," Antonio said. "We have a safehouse in Arezzo. Nothing like this, of course, but—''

"I have seen to it," Karpov said, again cutting off Martella. "The details are being worked out now. The hostages will be gone late this afternoon. The DiAlto mission shall proceed under the contingency plan.''

"And if we are attacked, is it worth the men we will lose?" Antonio asked.

"The assault on the house in Bellagio suggests the

work of an individual or a paramilitary group that prefers night work. It would seem that we have until tonight to deal with the matter of the traitor among us. We will kill that menace and be gone from here by twilight—perhaps we will be gone before the enemy has time to launch an attack.''

''I understand,'' Martella said. ''I will see to doubling the security here at the palace, just to be on the safe side, just in case they catch up to us sooner than we expect. An attack could come at any time.''

''That is the first intelligent thing you've said today. Let us tour the grounds. We will triple security measures. We will be ready for anything. Lead the way.''

Antonio went to the door and held it open for Karpov, keeping his eyes lowered so the Russian could not see the hatred that burned in them.

As the pair left the library, a three-man crew arrived to see to the removal of Libera's body.

Antonio eyed the crew and shook his head in disgust. He wondered what was going on behind Karpov's snake eyes. He wondered about the stability, the ruthlessness of Emilia Salerno. Before the day ended, Martella knew, more blood would run within the palace of Gaspare Savasta.

His mind was cluttered with black clouds of thought; but Antonio's main concern was not a cloud, it was a storm: a storm brought over his head by the man Emilia had slaughtered. That man, who was now being kicked off the carpet, had said only one man was responsible for the death of all those well-trained, professional fighters at Villa Savasta.

One man.

10

THE ATMOSPHERE IN THE office was thick with nerve-racking anticipation.

The offices of the Milan NOCS branch were located in a nondescript three-level gray stone building on the Via Ceresio, just a short jaunt from the Castello Sforzesco at Sempione Park in the heart of Milan.

Noonday sun squinted in through the windows of Captain Vianake's office. The sun cast patterns on the tile floor, catching and cutting clouds of cigarette smoke.

Road maps, weapons and charts were scattered throughout the room.

Vianake's office—and the offices of all his staff members—was located on the second floor of the government building. The first floor housed a large garage and arsenal. The top level was a detention area for political criminals.

Colonel DiAlto and Captain Vianake had just finished listening to Colonel John Phoenix and Gia Vallone deliver their report on the early-morning happenings at Villa Savasta in Bellagio.

Vianake, upon hearing the details, reassured the Americans that all possible steps were being taken by the Italian authorities to keep the media lid on both the Bellagio firefight and the kidnapping of DiAlto's family.

Vianake was a heavyset man with a huge barrel chest. When he spoke, it sounded as though his voice rumbled up from the depths of his stocky frame.

"So, as you see, my friends," he said, "at least we continue to operate behind a cloak of anonymity. Our men are combing the countryside, covertly of course. I am certain it will only be a matter of time before...."

DiAlto, occupying a chair facing Vianake, rose impatiently and interrupted him. "Only a matter of time before my wife and daughter are found in some goddamn ditch, slaughtered like animals. For all your talk, you're really not doing a damn thing."

Vianake was taken back by the verbal barrage. He cast a nervous glance around the room, his eyes landing on the nearest window. "Colonel, we all understand what you are going through. Believe me, we all care about the safety of your wife and daughter. We're doing everything in our power."

"But everything in your power does not appear to be enough," DiAlto countered, anger strangling his voice.

Colonel John Phoenix felt like hell. He felt like hell for the guy sitting across the room from him.

Sitting beside the window, he could feel the sun's warmth. He wished he could hand out that warmth and give it to a deserving soldier like Mike DiAlto.

"I know how you feel, Mike, but you've got to keep cool. You're a pro."

The words were spoken softly. But they registered.

DiAlto sank back in his chair and lit a cigarette.

"Sorry," he finally said, exhausted. "This thing's just tearing me up."

"It's tearing up all of us," Bolan said.

DiAlto took a long, calming drag off his smoke, then put his mind back on his job. "I've got the information you requested earlier," he said to Phoenix.

Bolan was about to tell him to dole out the information when an extra sense warned him against the idea. The big guy looked at Vianake.

"Captain, will you excuse us for a few minutes?"

The NOCS officer stood up from behind his desk. He gazed out the window once again, then left his desk and moved toward the office door.

"Of course, Colonel Phoenix. My orders were to give you full run of these facilities. I'm at your disposal. I will be waiting for you down the hall."

Vianake's eyes flickered toward the window. Then he departed, closing the door briskly behind him.

"Nervous as hell," DiAlto muttered, referring to Vianake.

"Maybe he's got a reason to be nervous," Bolan said.

Gia Vallone had been sitting, quietly observing the three-man exchange, adding little to the conversation. Finally she cut in.

"What about me, Colonel Phoenix?" she asked, her voice slightly bitter. She rose from her chair and walked toward Bolan. "You obviously do not trust Captain Vianake, and he is my immediate superior. In the car you questioned my loyalty. What now?"

Bolan allowed a slight grin. He admired the woman's bluntness, just as he admired her battle savvy.

"Maybe I didn't trust you one hundred percent. But on the drive here, I thought about what's happened. You had a loaded weapon at Bellagio, and you had a good chance to aim at my back. You didn't. Gia," he added, his gaze fixing her, "I've got that gut feeling."

Bolan then turned to DiAlto and asked: "Have you gone over this place for bugs?"

DiAlto nodded. "While Vianake was out of the office." He indicated a framed photograph of Italy's countryside that hung on a wall above a row of filing cabinets. "I found a transmitting unit behind it. I yanked it."

Gia Vallone was still torn between the two sides.

"But Colonel Phoenix," she said, "why should a hidden microphone indicate that Captain Vianake cannot be trusted? Surely you can appreciate bureaucratic procedure.''

"I can't appreciate anything about that man," Bolan said. "Listen, the only thing we've got on our side right now is time, and we don't have a whole lot of that. Are you with us, Gia? I want to keep this circle tight. You're initiated already," he said, indicating her bandaged shoulder wound. "I can sure use you as a backup on this. We can work together.''

Gia's brown eyes made contact with the big man's icy blues.

"I'm committed to you and to what happens next, Colonel. Count me in on your circle.''

Bolan fired his attention over to DiAlto.

"Okay, partner," he said, "what information did you dig up for us?''

"That place in Bellagio was the senator's vacation home for the ski season. His regular base is an ancestral estate in the Tuscany region outside of Florence.''

"Family?" Bolan asked.

"No. Wife died of cancer twelve years ago. They had a son and a daughter, but they're both grown and living somewhere—in the north we believe. Anyway, the ties have been severed.''

"And his ancestral estate, is that where you think we'll find your family?''

Pain stabbed DiAlto's face. He thought long and

hard on that question, but he never had a chance to give Bolan an answer.

Like lightning striking in a storm, Colonel John Phoenix was on his feet. Moving in a flash across the office, the big guy snatched Gia Vallone right off her feet.

DiAlto sat stunned.

"Get the hell out of here!" Bolan hollered. "Move!"

DiAlto, sitting next to the door, jumped from his chair and whipped open the office door, his combat sense now on alert.

Phoenix carried the startled Gia through the door.

"What the hell's going on?" DiAlto yelled.

Bolan replied, but DiAlto did not hear.

Glass shattered. The room shook.

DiAlto never made it out the door.

11

THE SURVIVAL INSTINCTS that Mack Bolan had honed in the jungles of Vietnam and had fine-tuned in his street war against the Mafia had grown more acute with each year, and every battle.

Sitting in the NOCS office of Captain Vianake, discussing the specifics of the Italian mission, those survival instincts had been working overtime, scanning the scene for anything out of place. He knew that danger was hiding near the office in the heart of Milan just as it lurked in the jungle and in the streets.

While the conversation had bounced between Vianake and DiAlto, Bolan had sat and watched the roof of the building located directly across from Vianake's office.

Bolan had noted that the roof ended at the same height as the office. Bolan also noted Vianake's constant glances out the window.

Minutes after Bolan had entered the conversation, while his senses remained on the building across the street, he saw the noonday sun flicker off metal on that roof. *Metal on that roof.*

That was when Mack Bolan had broken into action.

AS HE SPRINTED out of the office, he heard DiAlto fire a question. He began to answer on the run, but was interrupted by the boom of a grenade launcher.

"Get down," he ordered, burying Gia under him.

The incoming HE ruptured the glass window, striking the office with knockout power.

Looking back, Bolan saw Mike DiAlto caught in the doorway. The force of the shuddering blast pitched him, arms extended, into the opposite wall of the corridor. He rolled over onto his back, groaned, then blacked out.

The building came alive in response to the blast even before the loud echoes of horror had faded. Chaos. Bolan heard wild shouts from the upper level where convicted terrorists were detained.

Lifting himself off Gia, Bolan palmed the Auto-Mag, taking the death dealer from its holster. With speed in his stride, he reached Colonel DiAlto and crouched by his side.

DiAlto had an ugly gash near his left temple, but Bolan could detect no deeper wounds, no blood holes caused by slivers of shrapnel. DiAlto was dazed, bruised. But he was alive.

Regaining some clarity, DiAlto sat upright and leaned against the wall. He looked at Bolan, but his eyes still registered confusion.

"What the hell!" DiAlto said. "Did you get the number of that truck?"

Bolan laughed. His spirits were lifted with the survival of a fighting man.

"Truck, hell, it was a grenade attack from the building across the street—you only wish it was a truck," Bolan said. His tone became serious. "I didn't like the way Vianake kept looking out that window. It was like he was expecting something."

Gia came over beside the pair.

"You okay?" she asked DiAlto.

"Little shaken. But I'm okay." DiAlto tugged an army issue Colt .45 automatic from a concealed holster under his Class A uniform.

"What do you have in mind, Colonel?" he said.

Before Bolan could respond, another explosion rocked the building.

"You stay here and keep on top of what's happening," Bolan commanded Gia. "Get close as you can to Captain Vianake, then stick. Don't let the bastard out of your sight. But be careful."

Gia nodded, accepting Bolan as her leader.

Bolan was already moving away, speeding toward the door. "I'm taking out the grenade launcher."

"And I'm going with you," DiAlto replied, matching the Executioner step for step.

Distant reports of automatic weapons reached Bolan. NOCS personnel returning fire, he guessed. The fire was sporadic. This was the central business district of Milan. The government force would have to exercise extreme caution.

Bolan and DiAlto burst through a doorway leading to the emergency stairs. The Executioner heard another incoming burst land somewhere in the building.

A daylight attack in downtown Milan.

Nervy bastards, Bolan thought.

The big guy's attention was drawn toward the stairs leading to the floor above them. Bolan and DiAlto tracked their weapons to the stairway, waiting for the noisemakers to appear. Both held their fire.

Three men, in identical prisoner's garb, came barreling down the stairs, attempting to escape from the detention unit for terrorists. The trio toted guns and the prisoner in the middle held a .44 pistol across the throat of an unconscious prison guard.

The prisoners froze at the sight of Bolan and DiAlto. The man holding the guard shouted a command. The men flanking him tracked their weapons downward.

Bolan's right arm, extending the AutoMag, was a blur. Big Thunder chugged one of its death pills, nailing the middle prisoner in the forehead.

The prisoner was kicked back, stretching out across the width of the stairwell.

The unconscious prison guard collapsed and toppled down the stairs, stopping between Bolan and

DiAlto. The American pair were centering their attention on the two remaining escapees, who were flattening themselves against the stone wall of the stairwell while drawing beads on their opponents.

DiAlto took quick aim and made a mess of the guy on the left. The heavy pistol boomed in the narrow confines of the battleground.

The AutoMag in Bolan's fist blazed once more. The man he aimed at saw it coming. As he let out a scream, the 9mm bullet turned his throat into a bloody gash, his jugular vein severed. The prisoner flopped like a rag doll over the rail.

Save for the ringing that was in Bolan's ears, the stairwell was quiet. There were still tremors of activity coming from other parts of the building. But in the narrow hallway, there were only the two living amid an acrid smell of gunsmoke and death.

Mike DiAlto raced up a few steps to where one of the escapees lay wasted. He grabbed the guy's Uzi. The Uzi in hand, he holstered his .45.

Bolan took a look at the guard. It had been a bluff. The man was already dead. A gaping hole marked the back of his head. His body was already cool.

Gunfire rang out from within the corridor on the top floor, beyond their range of vision.

Bolan turned to DiAlto. ''They're trying to free the prisoners as well as hit us,'' he said.

As DiAlto nodded in agreement, three more prisoners piled through the doorway after escaping from the NOCS forces that were trying to contain them. The trio was not armed. That was their tough luck.

DiAlto opened up with the Uzi and took out two men in a quick cluster pattern that ripped guts and life from the toppling bodies.

Bolan cleaned up the scene, stroking the AutoMag, which responded with a well-placed puncture on the third guy's forehead. Blood spurted out. The prisoner knelt on the floor, then collapsed.

DiAlto charged up the stairs toward the upper-level battleground. In full stride, he called back to Bolan: "Go ahead. Get out there and nail that grenade launcher before the shitkicker knocks us into next week."

The NATO man disappeared through the doorway that led to the thick of the fight. Bolan heard DiAlto's announced entrance—the chattering of the Uzi.

Colonel John Phoenix reloaded the AutoMag and continued on his way.

He left the stairwell and entered the garage. Gunfire cracked above him, sounds of panic echoed through the building.

A dozen or more civilian and unmarked cars were parked in the garage, along with four armored personnel carriers and two tanklike urban assault vehicles.

A handful of armed commandos stood guard by the large double doors of the garage. The doors

opened onto a side street, now filled with people flee-
ing the scene of combat in front of the building.

The commandos' fighting instincts were as fine-
edged as Bolan's. Three of the men kept their eyes
riveted on the street. Another commando swung
around in a low crouch, his M-12 submachine gun
zeroing in on the Executioner.

"Identify yourself," the commando yelled in
Italian. "Who are—"

He was interrupted by squealing breaks and the
shouts of the other men.

Two cars had skidded to angled stops thirty feet
beyond the open garage doors. Terrorists were
stooped behind each car, opening up with automatic
weapons. Another two terrorists had fallen away
from the cars into prone positions and were also
opening fire on the garage.

The government men had seen it coming. They
whipped their M-12s into action. But they were
severely outmatched in manpower and firepower.

One commando had time to fire off a quick burst
from his machine gun. The burst disintegrated a side
window on one of the terrorist cars and took off a
hardguy's head.

But then the commando, and his partner beside
him, were lifted off their feet by the hail of stitching
lead from six automatic weapons. The pair landed in
dead heaps on the garage floor.

A third commando triggered off a burst from his

M-12, killing one of the terrorists with head-busting efficiency.

The commando then dodged back out of the terrorists' line of fire. The incoming projectiles bounced off everything but flesh and bone. The bullets buzzed in the garage like angry hornets.

The commando who had confronted Bolan still had his machine gun pointed in the Executioner's direction, although both men were forced to back away from the garage-door opening to escape the fire.

"DiAlto," Bolan snapped at the man. "Mike DiAlto."

He hoped that these words in the heat of battle would be enough for the NOCS man to trust him so they could join forces.

In the heartbeat before the commando could make his decision and respond, Bolan saw something over the man's shoulder, out in the street.

The civilians had long since taken cover. Bolan had a clear view of two terrorists yanking grenade pins and pitching the explosives through the double doors of the garage.

The Executioner executed a quick judo kick that snapped the barrel of the commando's M-12 away from his chest. He reached out, grabbed the front of the guy's jacket and pulled the commando down with him behind the bulk of the nearest armored personnel carrier.

Bolan was dealing with a highly trained combat man. But before the commando could recover, the garage of NOCS headquarters shuddered from the terrorist grenades. The explosion was a thunderclap of dire destruction.

12

BOLAN AND THE NOCS COMMANDO were showered with debris. With the echoes of the blast fading, the Executioner discerned the sound of car doors slamming and engines tearing away from the scene.

The commando and Bolan pushed themselves to their feet and rushed across the smoking garage. The men ran through the clutter of machinery that had taken the brunt of the blast.

The commando gave Bolan a curt nod. He knew now that they were on the same side, they were working together.

The defender by the doors had not been so lucky. His corpse was propped up against one wall. He looked like a freshly gutted animal.

Bolan and the commando ran out into the sunny street to see both hit cars roar away in opposite directions.

Bolan and the Italian anti-terrorist stood back-to-back in the center of the narrow side street. The pair had only one chance and they knew it: hope for a perfect shot.

The big guy adopted a shooting-range stance. He aimed and fired.

His ears were filled with the chatter of the M-12 machine gun being fired by the commando behind him. But his eyes were full of the car he aimed at.

Bolan's bullet pierced the back right tire. The auto swerved slightly. Bolan fired again. The car lost what little control remained. It plowed into a brick building with phenomenal force. Within seconds of impact, the car was enveloped in a fireball that blew out windows.

Bolan glanced over his shoulder. The commando at his back had crippled the other getaway. Figures were spilling from that car.

An agonized scream brought the big guy's attention back to the car he had sent sailing into the wall. Bolan saw a figure covered in flames, stumbling from the fire, shrieking in terror. The Executioner erased the agony with a mercy shot.

No one else emerged from the fiery wreck. The car and the terrorists were being eaten alive by flames.

Bolan turned to check on the Italian commando's action. Three men had emerged from the car and were cautiously advancing toward the commando, who stood covering them with his M-12. He ordered them to halt and place their hands on their heads.

The Executioner saw something the NOCS man was obviously blind to: a fourth terrorist had left the wreckage and was crawling around the side of the car that faced away from the commando's vision. The hardguy was carrying a MAC-11 machine pistol, and his aim was centered on the skull of the commando.

Big Thunder tracked around and down. The gun chugged almost unnoticed amid the roar of battle still raging around the front of the building. Another hit sounded from the grenade launcher as the hardguy with the MAC-11 rolled over, his face having absorbed the force of the bullet.

The three terrorists heard their buddy drop his weapon and that cued them into action. They broke their loose formation, no longer feigning surrender. They scattered like flies, tugging pistols from belt holsters.

Bolan continued the arm sweep that had taken out the terrorist behind the car. The AutoMag fired again, sending a 9mm punch that knocked one of the hardguys over with a blow to the temple. The guy dropped in a lifeless pile.

The NOCS man grunted in sudden pain. Bolan heard the sound, looked over and saw his commando fighting partner drop to the ground, clutching a painful leg wound as the two remaining terrorists opened fire, whistling a storm of bullets toward them.

The Executioner triggered the AutoMag two more times as he went into a weave pattern, making himself a more elusive target.

Another terrorist felt the wrath of Bolan's blasts when two holes slapped into his head.

Avoiding the last living terrorist's bullets, Bolan
sprawled into a shoulder roll. He figured he was on
his own now, his partner felled by the bastards. But
the big guy was wrong.

The NOCS commando, ignoring his leg wound,
triggered off a short burst from his machine gun that
sent the final terrorist reeling in a misty cloud of
blown-apart flesh. The remains of the guy toppled
into the gutter.

Bolan raced over to the commando. He helped the
guy to his feet. The thigh wound was open, raw.

The American warrior motioned that he had to
continue the battle on other fronts. The guard
nodded that he understood. Bolan tapped his brother
soldier lightly on the shoulder as a sign of gratitude
and respect, and left the Italian to defend the ground
he lay on should anyone be foolhardy enough to try
and claim it.

Bolan walked beside the building's outside wall
until he came to the corner at the main thoroughfare
that fronted the structure. He paused to reload. He
glanced around the corner, looking up at the position
where the grenade launcher sat.

There had been no explosions from incoming grenades for more than a minute. Sirens raged in the distance. Bolan wondered if the terrorist force was
withdrawing, quitting the scene.

He left the cover of the NOCS building in a dash to
the base of the facing building. Several commandos

were emerging from the government building, commencing a cautious advance on the building across the street. Bolan saw a get-away van parked close to the scene, its engine running.

The Executioner reached the corner of the building at the exact moment that a door on the side of the building was drawn inward.

Three terrorists, two men and a woman, came out of the building, heading for the van and carrying an RPG-7 grenade launcher.

They saw Bolan. Bolan saw them.

Reaction on both sides was spontaneous.

The terrorists dropped the grenade launcher and reached for their side arms.

The AutoMag bucked. A terrorist was caught by the bullet, his right nostril exploding with the impact. The guy's knees turned to melting butter. He collapsed.

The Executioner went into a forward fall. He landed stretched out on the pavement, returning fire. His ears picked up the sound of the van's engine as it cranked into life.

The woman fired. Chips of pavement laced Bolan's face; razor-thin slices of concrete crossed his cheek, just missing his right eye.

Bolan returned the fire. The bullet slammed the blonde backward out of her crouch. As she lay on her back, her hair took on a reddish tint.

The van started to pull away. The big guy knew he

had to let the wheelman go. His concentration was focused on the third terrorist who was still firing wildly.

Bolan took a shot. Missed. The guy was moving, trying to make his escape. Bolan tracked the hardguy. On the run, the man died, a 9mm skullbuster parked in his head. The guy did a short dance of death before crashing to the pavement.

As quick as the man fell, Bolan was noting the new action in the street.

A fire-engine red Ferrari had blocked the van's escape route at the end of the side street.

The driver of the van, an older, hard-looking hood, bailed out of the passenger side of the van with an Uzi machine gun rapping out a heavy stream of projectiles at the Ferrari.

The driver of the sports car was not wasting any time on formalities. As the Ferrari's windshield disappeared in a shower of safety glass, he took cover behind the slick car.

The man leaned around the side of the car, letting loose with a splattering spray of slugs from an Ingram machine pistol and Bolan smiled in recognition.

The guy's slugs had been perfectly placed, knocking the hardguy to the ground and jabbing the corpse along the cobblestones. And then the man with the Ingram straightened from behind the sports car and walked toward Bolan.

The newcomer wore a satisfied grin. Despite the

gray circumstances surrounding their meeting, Bolan could not contain a loud greeting.

"Welcome to Italy, Leo. They say it always gets a little crazy around here during the tourist season."

The two men connected with a warm handshake that carried deep feelings of friendship and mutual respect—respect born and raised in many miles of thunder and blood.

The man was Leo Turrin.

Turrin's closeness to Mack Bolan dated back to their crime-fighting association in the infancy of the Executioner's war against the Mafia.

Turrin was about the last man on earth that Bolan had expected to see on this battle turf.

"Good to have you aboard," Bolan said, the grin still on his face.

"Good to be here," Turrin said with a knowing smile.

In reality, Turrin knew that it was never good to be where the Executioner was. Around Mack Bolan lurked a constant cloud of risk. The cloud carried the rains of death. But Leo Turrin also knew that what Mack Bolan did was essential for man's survival.

"Good to be here," he repeated.

13

LEO TURRIN. A hell of a friend. An ally. A fighter who would kick ass from Tuscany to Tucson for a cause—a good cause like the DiAlto kidnappings.

Bolan sat with Leo, Colonel DiAlto and Gia Vallone at an outdoor café along the Via Monte Rose, less than a quarter of a mile from the NOCS government building that had been attacked.

The foursome sat at a corner table that was nestled between two manicured hedges, offering them privacy, the privacy they needed to talk and plan.

At the NOCS building, the damage was still being assessed.

The Red Column had notified the media of their "heroic attempt to free political prisoners." The yellow-backs failed to mention that the mass jail-break was stopped in progress and that no prisoners escaped. They also failed to mention the DiAlto affair.

The media got a hold of the body count: five NOCS personnel, seven prisoners and fourteen Red Column terrorists. A major engagement. An estimate of the damage to the building was still unavailable, but obviously high.

Stress was carved into the face of each person at the table. It had been that kind of day. That kind of week.

Leo Turrin tried to keep his companions at ease with talk; he was never at a loss for words. Mack Bolan listened to those words and let them lull him into reflections of the past.

Leo Turrin had been one of the Executioner's first targets in the opening campaign in Mack Bolan's war against the Mafia. The war had opened in Bolan's hometown of Pittsfield, Massachusetts, when the young soldier, hot from the hellgrounds of Nam, had returned stateside to bury his family—innocent victims of Mob terror. After the burial, Mack Bolan had set his steely sights on the Mob and he gave himself a goal: to blow away every Mafia *capo* he could find.

The first *capo* he came across was Leo "The Pussy" Turrin.

It had taken some damn fast talking and some gutsy action by Leo's wife to save Turrin's ass and convince the Executioner that Leo was in fact one of the U.S. government's highest-placed undercover agents in the Justice Department's organized crime division.

Leo and Bolan the blitz-artist had been glued in friendship ever since.

Leo's agent-in-place status had been elevated in the Mob hierarchy—aided along the way by well-orchestrated Bolan hits—until Turrin was placed on the Mob's ruling board, *La Commissióne*. As a member of the board, the undercover agent had a handle on the inside track of the Mob's activities.

Turrin continued his potentially deadly role as a kingpin in the Mob's Manhattan boardrooms; it was a role he still held even as he was talking over a coffee in the outdoor café.

"An eager-beaver buddy of Hal Brognola's pieced it together over at Justice," Turrin was saying. "I picked it up from Porksy Lassetti and Erno Guzik at a board meeting two days ago.

"They've all known about Savasta's joint in Tuscany for more than six months. I should've heard about it earlier, but they kept the lid on it except for a tight little circle—guess they didn't see the need to broadcast. But sooner or later we had to find out. I passed it on to Justice and Hal's man added it all up and fed it back to him."

"What about Lassetti and Guzik?" Bolan asked.

"Runners. Bottom rung. Street work for Telly Smaldone. We of *La Commissióne* passed down a friendly reminder to Telly, telling him to fork over past percentages plus interest. He complied.

"Smaldone has been selling guns over here and picking up on laundered Russian and East German black money through Savasta's dump outside Florence. That's how these Red Column boys and girls have been financing themselves. Lassetti and Guzik made the run every fifteen days.''

"What did those guys say about the operation?'' Bolan wanted to know. "Do we have a reading on what kind of force we're up against?''

"At least a small, tight army. The people at Savasta's palace kept Lassetti and Guzik pretty high and happy while they were visiting, so neither remembers much. But they were impressed with the hard security.

"And Guzik remembers the boss there, a guy named Martella, bragging to hell about how the palace had been turned into a 'people's prison' for the Red Justice Column.''

Colonel Mike DiAlto, trying to piece together all he had learned, glanced at the man he knew to be Colonel John Phoenix.

"You had me running down that site in Tuscany before you got back from Bellagio.''

"I knew the Red Column had its claws into Savasta,'' Bolan said. "There's no reason why they wouldn't use the senator again if they could. This guy Martella's got a right to brag. No one would suspect the ancestral digs of a far-left senator to be used as a hardsite for urban guerrillas. Until now. Thanks for filling in the blanks, Leo. That's the place where they're holding the hostages.''

"They won't stay there for long,'' Gia noted grimly. "We must move quickly. I know these people, I know how they think. They will be making plans to move the hostages again, as they did from Bellagio—if they haven't moved them already."

"Leo's intel is good enough for me," DiAlto said, his impatience boiling over. "Let's quit wasting time sitting on our butts. Let's hit the damn palazzio in Tuscany before they move my family again."

"Hang on, Mike," Bolan said, "you're getting ahead of us again. Leo's got more."

Bolan turned to his old buddy. "Hal got back to you after his friend at Justice passed along that intel about the palace in Tuscany, right?"

"He did," Turrin said. "Here's how we're set up—by the way, it's Hal's scenario from the git-go.

"I put through a transatlantic call yesterday morning from New York to this guy, Martella, who's a big gun at the senator's place.

"My line to them is that I represent the Smaldone family of New York, and that I have proof of a cop infiltration of the Red Justice Column. For a damn good price, Martella's people think they're flying me over here to finger the undercover agent. I supposedly know the fink and can identify him."

"And there's no truth to any of it," Bolan remarked.

"None," Turrin said. "It's all total crap. But it will serve as the in you need to get close to the hostages—Martella expects me to have a bodyguard traveling with me.'' His eyes collided with the cold gaze of Mack Bolan.

The pair posted the thumbs-up sign.

Gia Vallone leaned forward. Concern almost buried her voice. ''But that would be a suicide mission for you,'' she said softly to Bolan and Turrin. ''You would be caught in the enemy's den, cut off from the outside.''

''The lady's right,'' grunted DiAlto. ''It won't do anyone any bloody good if you guys walk in there and get killed. What's wrong with hitting them full strength?''

''My guess is that the Column is entrenched into that palace hideout even harder than they were at Bellagio,'' Bolan said. ''With the two of us working alone, we'll have a better chance of getting to Louise and Angel as any daylight frontal assault. A soft penetration like this is the only way to go, Mike. A hard penetration may make the bastards trigger-happy with your family.''

DiAlto inhaled the logic and came to understand all of Bolan's reasoning. But he was a man nearly consumed by inner torment.

''There's got to be something I can do,'' he insisted. ''We're talking about my family.''

''There is something you can do,'' Bolan assured him. ''The second most important element in this is Captain Vianake. He set us up in his office. The guy's obviously a paid contact of the Red Justice Column.''

"I accept your assessment of Vianake, Colonel Phoenix," Gia said. "I'm sorry it took me so long to be convinced. But why did you suspect Vianake before the attack at his office?"

Bolan nodded to DiAlto.

"It was a fresh lead from Mike that sent me to contact a Column fink named Ciucci when I arrived here in Italy yesterday. Only Mike and Vianake knew I had gone to Como to meet Ciucci, and why. Ciucci would have made damn sure he wasn't followed to our meeting, and, of course, so did I. Still, a Column hit squad nailed Ciucci just after he arrived. How did the bastards know where and when Ciucci was going to spill his guts? Vianake. That snake Vianake."

"So you want me to keep an eye on Vianake while you take off to Tuscany," DiAlto stated. "Why can't Gia take care of that?"

Mack Bolan seldom took time for explanations. He was not a talker, not like his friend Leo, but the big guy knew that talk was cheap and, for such a cheap price, talk could buy a good soldier some peace.

"Listen, Mike, the Red Justice Column is about to find this thing coming down like a noose around their necks. Vianake will have to make direct contact with them and everyone's going to be jumping. Since we let her sit in on our meeting, Vianake probably knows where Gia's loyalty lies. Besides, Gia has already taken a bullet. She'll be able to provide backup for us, but we need an able-bodied soldier on Vianake.''

The NATO man accepted the strategy. ''Okay, Colonel, I'll get back to what's left of Vianake's office right now.''

''We'd all better get moving,'' Bolan said. ''Remember Mike, Vianake is important and dangerous. Don't give these guys an opening. Don't give them any room to breathe.''

DiAlto was up and on his way toward the NOCS building, nodding crisply to the man who was risking his neck for the sake of DiAlto's family.

Bolan watched DiAlto leave. ''There goes a damn good man,'' he said. ''One of the hard ones.''

Gia Vallone surveyed the two men still sitting at the table with her. ''You are all good men,'' she said.

Bolan touched Gia's arm in a gesture of graciousness. The lady was all class, he thought. He was glad he had gotten that gut feeling about her. She was on his side, that was for sure.

The Executioner lifted himself to his feet.

''Let's take it to Tuscany,'' Leo Turrin said.

''Let's *hit* Tuscany,'' Bolan added.

14

From Mack Bolan's journal

There is a plague running wild in our world that threatens to wipe out everything man has achieved after centuries of struggle against the forces of brutality.

A sickness has spread its infection of violence and revolution so widely over our planet that no nation is untouched by it today.

Man, without morality, is an animal.

And the animalism of man has exploded upon the civilized world in a frenzy of murder.

Pick up today's newspaper or watch tonight's television news program and you'll see and hear the latest outrages in a world infected with the virus of terrorism.

It's a plague compounded of ruthless greed, egotistical vanity and brutal personal ambition. It lives on a burning desire for power, and a total disregard for the rights of others to live without hurt or harm.

So, yeah, there's a war going on between moral man and animal man. A war fought on their side with kidnappings and murders and assassinations. Blowing up a busload of school kids. Gunning down priests.

They not only kill, they have corrupted good words like "freedom," and "patriotism" and "martyr." They call themselves "freedom fighters" or "the liberation party," and the rest of us are afraid to call them what they are: murderers.

What in hell has happened to this world?

If you saw one man gun down another on your street corner, you'd call the cops because he's a killer.

But when you see on your television set a few guys dressed in patched-up uniforms and watch them machine-gun down a score of innocent bystanders... or, if you see pictures of oily smoke rising from burning schools and close-ups of the sprawled corpses of women and children lying in bright red pools of their own blood, and the camera then cuts to some creep in a beret clutching an automatic rifle high in the air with one hand and he's spouting off some crap about how he's fighting oppression and destroying injustice, you don't know what to think.

Famous television personalities give him the dignity of "objective" interviews in which they never question the bullshit he's spouting. Even though his hands are dripping blood from his helpless victims, he claims he's not a killer because he's fighting for a "cause."

Yeah, he's supposed to be fighting for liberty—but

he's depriving others of their liberty while he's doing it.

He's fighting oppression by oppressing the helpless who cannot fight back.

He shoots some guy's kneecaps off, crippling him for life, and he talks about eliminating "injustice."

He rants about "class struggle" and how he's fighting for the downtrodden.

It's time we looked behind the self-important labels these animals place on themselves and call them what they are.

Terrorists. Murderers. Killers. Animals.

They're clever. They're smart enough to exploit other men to achieve their own ends. They're vicious, callous and eager to kill so long as it brings them more publicity and notoriety.

Somehow, the money they steal—the millions of dollars in ransom, the billions of dollars if they succeed in taking over a country—never gets to help the poor.

And the poor continue to be poor and desperate. They live as miserably as they did before—only under a different set of dictators.

Animal man has been, and always will be, my enemy. I'm not afraid to stand up to him and call him what he is. I'll put a bullet in his head just as fast as he'd put one in mine if I gave him the chance.

For sure. I intend to fight animal man to the final, bloody end—his or mine.

No, I'm not his judge or jury or prosecutor. I don't have to be. His own acts of kill-crazy violence makes him guilty as hell.

All I am is his Executioner.

A .44 Magnum slug in the brainpan of a murderer is the fastest way I know of to end his threat to the peace of ordinary people.

There are others who feel the same way I do. Who have sworn to lay down their lives if they have to, to defend and protect what generations of moral man have fought and bled and died for—the right of the individual to live without fear of violence.

If guys like us don't fight them, who will?

15

Two "REPRESENTATIVES FROM NEW YORK" secretly connected with a commercial flight from the United States at the Milan airport.

One of those men was Leo "The Pussy" Turrin, a main man in the Mob, and the other was Turrin's bodyguard, Nick.

The pair disembarked amid a planeload of tourists and businessmen when the flight touched down in Florence.

Stepping off the plane, Leo Turrin turned to his longtime friend, Mack Bolan, and instructed him as to his duties. "Nick," he said, smiling ear to ear. "Your job is to protect me. Do it."

"Clown," was all Bolan said in reply.

Leo knew exactly where to find a shiny new Lancia in the crowded airport parking lot. He was a visiting dignitary, and the appropriate arrangements had been made with his knowledge and involvement.

The pair had not been able to take weapons on the commercial airplane, so Leo had made sure his "friends" provided him with all the hardware he and his bodyguard would need.

Opening the trunk of the Lancia, Turrin showed Bolan a suitcase.

Anyone attempting to open the suitcase without the proper key and combination would have been blown skyward.

Leo opened the suitcase. For himself he took out an old-fashioned .45. A full array of death-dealing equipment was stashed in the suitcase for Bolan.

With his "boss" in the passenger's seat, Nick negotiated his way through the streets of Florence, a city one-fourth the size of Milan. The streets were tree-lined and the pace of life was markedly slower in contrast to the high-paced life of the industrial north.

Traveling along the river Arno, which bisects the southern end of Florence, Bolan battled the speed-happy Italian motorists.

The Lancia crossed the river on the shop-lined fourteenth-century bridge called the Ponte Vecchio. Bolan steered the car onto the Via De Serragli, which turned into the highway to Siena. Soon they left behind the suburbs of Florence and took on the un-dulating agricultural terrain of rural Tuscany.

"Postcard country," Leo thought aloud.

"It's a great looking area," Bolan agreed. "But it's crawling with vermin."

Bolan and Turrin had gone over their strategy several times with Gia Vallone before they parted in

Milan. Much of the plan, they agreed, would have to be improvised.

Thirty miles south of Florence, Bolan guided the Lancia off the highway onto a country road that rolled across seemingly endless vineyards. Eventually they passed through the village of Poggibonsi.

The Latin faces that Bolan saw were granitelike, etched with pride and inner strength. The faces he saw were the faces of simple people who spent their lives working the land.

The Lancia sped through an area of timeless beauty. Poggibonsi disappeared behind them as the terrain grew more hilly. Terraced vineyards stretched for as far as the eye could see.

The car reached the top of a steep hill and Leo pointed out the target.

"There it is," he said. "Savasta's den."

Approaching Gaspare Savasta's Tuscany mansion from high ground, Bolan copped a long look at the layout of the place before the road dipped again.

The massive estate made Savasta's summer home in Bellagio seem like the dwelling of a small-time farmer.

Surrounded by a high stone wall, the palace stood on a terraced hillside overlooking a valley and facing Siena, barely visible on the southern horizon. The huge old structure was two stories beneath a low gabled roof.

Bolan could make out an open-air rectangular court, surrounded by tall pines. One sign of the modern world—a single-engine jet turbine Bell UH-D "Huey" helicopter, perched on a landing pad behind the palace—stuck out of the days-gone-by setting.

His mental maps carved out and stored in his memory, Bolan wheeled the Lancia off the road and onto the long winding approach to the front gate.

"Here we go. Good luck, guy," Leo said, sucking in a deep, relaxing breath.

Bolan, checking the looseness of his borrowed Beretta 92-S in its oiled holster, shot a glance at his friend. "Thanks for setting this up, Leo," he said. He meant it both ironically and sincerely. The semiautomatic 9mm handgun was one of Italy's newest, and Bolan was grateful for it. The *caratteristiche* or "character" of this weapon was something of a relief after the arm- numbing qualities of the AutoMag and the boxiness of the 93-R. This new pistol was light, incredibly compact—of *estrema compattezza* as Leo had put it—and had an oscillating block in the locking system that made it dead right for high-power ammunition. On the ride, Leo had waxed lyrical about the handgun's crisp and progressive trigger pull, or "*elevata dolcezza di scatto....*"

The entrance to the grounds was set dead center in the southern wall. The wall was topped with barbed wire and broken shards of glass were embedded in the stone. An iron-grille gate barred entrance.

The gate opened mechanically. The Lancia passed through.

A brick guardhouse stood just inside the wall. The station was manned by three guys in standard terrorist commando garb. Two of the hardguys were barely out of their teens—but they looked tough and mean with their Galil assault rifles—and there was an older man who wore a side arm holstered at his hip. The older guy was obviously in charge of the gate-watchers.

The pair of younger sentries stood blocking the driveway that led toward the castle. They held their weapons at port arms.

The Executioner brought the Lancia to a halt. He and Leo stepped from the car, each carrying an air of bored protocol.

"Turrin. Leo Turrin from New York. This is my associate Nick Bonoselli. Signor Martella is expecting us."

Turrin dipped his fingers into the side pocket of his jacket, slowly and with sufficient caution that no one would think he was reaching for a weapon. He withdrew a white envelope and extended it to the crew boss.

"It's a letter from Signor Smaldone to Signor Martella," Leo told the guy.

The crew boss palmed the envelope. He tallied a quick glance at Leo and Bolan, matched them with photos that he carried on a clipboard, then handed the letter back to Leo unopened.

"This letter is not my business," he said. "You

can deliver the letter to Antonio yourself. You may proceed, but first give us your weapons. You can have them back when you leave.''

Leo fired the guy a hot stare. "Stuff it, buddy." He turned back toward the car. "Better get your boys out of our way. I don't want Nick to have to run them over."

The head man dropped his clipboard as the younger sentries stepped forward.

"I have my orders," the older guy said. "You must give me your weapons before you continue."

The sentries were young. They were also inexperienced. They got too close.

Bolan swung a foot full-force into the crotch of the closest guard, kicking balls high up into areas meant for other organs.

The kid howled, dropped, rolled back and forth, retching between moans.

The big guy followed through, knocking the second sentry's rifle out of the man's grasp with one arm, while his other hand slid under his jacket and came out with the Beretta 92-S tracking in tight target acquisition as the crew boss was in the process of drawing his side arm.

Bolan fired. A pencil-flame and a parabellum slug cored the older guy through the bridge of his nose. He backpedaled into a clump of bushes, where he died in a bed of roses.

Nick Bonoselli, living up to his billing as the meanest bodyguard, pressed the hot snout of the Beretta against the right temple of the remaining guard.

"Seems there's been a change in orders," Bolan grunted. "Looks like we're keeping our guns. You want to phone your boss and tell him what happened—tell them that we're coming up? Or do you want me to blow away your head? Just nod if you want to live."

The guard nodded. A real quick nod.

Bolan marched the sentry into the guardhouse with Leo keeping pace. The guard made the call as Bolan clutched him with a near-choking grip.

The call completed, the sentry hung up the phone.

"Antonio doesn't like it. But you may proceed."

"Thanks," Leo said. "You've been really helpful."

Bolan delivered a quick, hard chop to the man's head and he dropped in a heap.

Bolan and Leo left the guardhouse. They returned to the Lancia and hopped in, Bolan taking his place behind the wheel. He slipped the car into gear and they continued up the driveway toward the medieval pallazzio.

The confrontation at the front gate had been anticipated by Bolan and Turrin. The outcome, Bolan knew, had added punch to the effectiveness of their penetration.

They were in.

Getting out—alive *and* with the DiAltos—was now their biggest problem.

16

LEO TURRIN, Antonio Martella and Viktor Karpov
sat in expensive antique chairs, nursing long-
stemmed glasses of wine.

Mack Bolan, in keeping with his role, stood re-
spectfully apart from the others. Bolan took this luxury of distance and used it to his advantage, scanning
the room, observing every detail.

Bolan had not been at all surprised by the presence
of a Russian KGB operative. Karpov was not intro-
duced as such, but the Executioner had caught the
man's true colors.

As Bolan surveyed the scene, Karpov surveyed Leo
and Martella. The KGB man remained cool and
aloof to the other two, and he totally ignored Nick.
But Karpov's shiny reptilian eyes missed nothing.

Martella was the opposite of Karpov. Martella
wanted it known that he was the *boss*. In fact he was
not the boss—he would jump at the snapping of Karpov's fingers.

Bolan noted that Martella's face wore the marks of
stress. He was obviously a young man with some-

thing pressing on his mind; he was living in an undercurrent of tension that he could not shake.

Standing in his pose as Leo's bodyguard, Bolan mused on what must be bothering Martella. The bastard was probably having his ass hounded for the little problem his boys had bought at Bellagio, Bolan thought. And it would be a man like Karpov who would provide such butt biting.

Martella, tried to keep the conversation light.

"Wine has been made here for at least a thousand years," he was saying. "The senator's ancestors built this palace in 1044. His family can be traced back to this area to at least 770."

"And where is Savasta?" Leo asked. "Guzik and Lassetti said he was around half the time they were here. I was half hoping to meet the guy. He sounds like a man to know in this country. I like to know the right people."

Martella was about to reply, but he was cut off by Karpov's monotone voice.

"Never mind Senator Savasta, Mr. Turrin," Karpov's monotonous voice cut in. "You are here to assist us in a vital matter. I suggest we begin."

Leo appraised Karpov with an openly antagonistic stare. Then he glanced at Bolan and gave a mean chuckle.

"Damn, Nick. They sure grow them direct and to the point in Russia, don't they? Too direct. Too to the point."

Bolan nodded, making no secret of his right hand hovering near the front of his jacket in Mafia bodyguard style.

Leo glared at Karpov and Martella. His feeling for the scum he was looking at came through in his eyes. "Something was said about $50,000."

"You shall receive payment after you identify the party you say is an infiltrator," Martella said.

"I'll have the money *now*," Turrin snarled. "Get it or you get nothing from me. It's no skin off my ass if I just turn around and drive back to the airport. You boys can take your chances."

"It seems you Americans prefer directness as well," Karpov said. "Very well, Mr. Turrin. Antonio. The money."

Martella disappeared from the room. The three men did not converse. Within minutes, Martella returned with a black leather briefcase. He handed the case to Turrin.

Leo tossed the case to his bodyguard. "Check it," he said.

Bolan caught the briefcase in his left hand, his right hand never leaving the vicinity of the Beretta. His eyes remained on Martella and Karpov.

Setting the briefcase on a glass-topped table, he snapped it open. The other three men watched him closely as he ran a thumb down two of the neatly packed stacks of crisp American dollars.

"Count it?" he asked Turrin.

"No. Just keep it with you. For your sake, I trust you guys," Turrin said, turning to the terrorist chiefs. "Now let's get started. I want a tour of this dump. I want a look at every face you boys have working for you—"

Turrin's sentence was snapped off by a woman who came striding into the room.

"Antonio," she said. "The hostages are ready to be moved. I want to...."

The rest of the sentence died as the woman's eyes caught Leo Turrin and Mack Bolan.

Bolan recognized her from the data that Leo had brought from New York—intel squeezed from Lassetti and Guzik after their visits to Tuscany.

Her name was Emilia Salerno. She was outfitted like her fellow "freedom" fighters: dark sweater, jeans and boots. She wore a Czech Scorpion auto-pistol low on her right hip.

Antonio Martella's eyes shone with renewed hatred as she entered the room.

"Emilia, you loudmouthed fool!"

Emilia Salerno's face turned pale. "I did not know your guests had arrived," she said. "May I speak with you alone, Antonio?"

"No. I want you to take these gentlemen on a tour of the castle and grounds."

She glared at Turrin and Bolan and then back at her boss. "But my charges," she said. "The deadline. I see no reason to wait—"

"Enough," Martella snarled. "You will obey me, Emilia. Do as I say. Now."

The woman turned her glare toward Bolan and Leo. Hostility shone from her dark eyes. "Come with me, *gentlemen*," she said, adding a sarcastic emphasis to the last word.

Leo and Bolan followed her as she left the room. Leo turned and gave Martella and Karpov a curt thumbs-up sign. "Consider your bad apple in the bag," he said. "We'll have the fink pinned when we get back."

Martella stood with his fists clenched. His mouth was an angry slit. The Red Column crew boss looked like he would give anything to wrap a fist around the Luger holstered at his hip. He stared at Emilia Salerno's back, his eyes blazing a path.

Cross currents were pulling at each other within the room, Bolan thought. A little hate within the ranks could always be turned to their advantage....

17

THE EXECUTIONER HAD WITNESSED the dying breaths of more men and women than any person should expect to in several lifetimes. In his journeys, Mack Bolan had picked up a theory: certain dwellings absorb much of what has taken place within their walls—the good, the bad, life and death.

Savasta's palace, pocketed some thirty miles south of Florence in Tuscany, was just such a place. Any army, ancient or modern, that had marched in this area of Tuscany had found the huge mansion in its path. Countless men of war had fought battles for it; and, for many, the battle had ended there, the blood dripping slowly off the final pages of their lives.

Within the confines of the palace, Leo Turrin and Emilia Salerno commenced their tour in search of a traitor who did not even exist except in Turrin's imagination. History surrounded the pair. Mack Bolan followed them.

There was little conversation between the trio as Emilia, grudgingly doing her duty, showed them all of the security measures that had been taken in the ancient building.

Bolan, still toting the briefcase full of money, filed the information for later reference.

The tour took thirty minutes. Bolan and Turrin were supposedly scrutinizing every face they saw. In reality, the two "Mafia" men were carefully assessing the placement of security personnel and firepower and the strengths and weaknesses of the fortress.

Bolan counted thirty Red Justice Column foot soldiers. In addition, there was the deadly inner circle of Martella, Karpov and Emilia and perhaps some other heavies.

Martella's guard force was every bit as well armed as the force Bolan had encountered in Bellagio. Bolan noted a wide range of weapons; the most popular side arm seemed to be the Scorpion autopistol. There were Uzis, many AK-47s and Galils, Heckler & Koch MP5K SD A3 submachine guns equipped with telescoping stocks and built-in noise suppressors, worn in shoulder straps and held in against the body.

When Emilia's tour was completed, Bolan knew one thing for certain: the place was *hard*.

Anticipation was lying just below the surface of everything he saw. Bolan had been a warrior long enough to recognize what was happening. Martella's outfit was ready to pull out.

That jibed with the reference Emilia had spilled about the moving of the hostages.

While the Executioner had a good overview of the defenses protecting the place, he also had a good idea where the hostages were being held.

Emilia had avoided taking Nick and Leo down one wing of the structure. She might just as well have pointed to the area and informed the pair that that's where the hostages were being held—avoiding the area completely had made it that obvious.

Antonio Martella and the KGB man, Karpov, were waiting for them when they returned. They had not budged.

"Have you seen everyone to your satisfaction, gentlemen?" Martella asked.

"I guess," grunted Leo. "Not that it matters a damn. If you want to know the truth, I had your fink pegged before I got here."

Martella raised a hand of caution. He looked at the woman.

"Emilia. Out. Please. You are correct, the deadline has passed. You may proceed."

The woman's pasty cheeks took on some color.

"Yes, Antonio. Right away."

Emilia turned and departed without a backward look.

It was coming down the pike now, Bolan thought. That sick bitch Emilia could not be allowed to touch Louise or Angel.

When the woman was gone, Viktor Karpov turned his cold eyes onto Leo.

"I understand you to be a direct man, Mr. Turrin. You have had your diversion, you've had your tour and you've had our guards thrown in the dirt. Enough is enough. Who is the infiltrator within the Red Column ranks?"

Turrin played it to the hilt. The VIP from the Big Apple chuckled without humor, then looked at Bolan, feeding the big guy the straight line.

"Hear that, Nick? Mr. Big ain't figured it out yet. Break the news to him."

Bolan eyed the two men, holding suspense on a razor's edge.

Finally he pointed an accusing finger at the man who stood beside Karpov.

"You're the man," the Executioner said to Antonio Martella. "You're a goddamn CIA agent."

18

LOUISE DIALTO HAD NO IDEA how long she and her daughter had been held captive in the windowless room. Time could not be counted or measured when each second registered only dull terror in the mind.

The Red Column thugs had amputated her finger soon after her and her daughter's abduction. That gruesome event seemed as though it had happened a lifetime ago.

The terrorists had rendered her unconscious—using a rag doused in chloroform—the moment they had been captured and whisked into the van during a shopping trip.

Louise's next sensation was that of being ripped from the womb of unconsciousness by a sense-shredding explosion of pain.

A woman had committed the atrocity...with no anesthetic save that first small dose that had knocked her out earlier. Then she had crudely bandaged the hand.

And Angel had been forced to watch.

The child's eyes mirrored unspeakable horror as

Louise had writhed in pain, shrieking as cold metal made contact with flesh.

At first Louise did not think she would be able to live with the pain. They changed the bandage once. Only once. Even when they moved her and Angel, she had not been offered anything to kill the pain.

One consolation continued to rise in Louise DiAlto's mind: at least, thank God, they had not touched her Angel.

Louise had spent all of Angel's life trying not to be overly protective. Still, Louise had learned that protectiveness was part of parenthood.

Angel, and her husband Mike, constituted her life.

Feelings of love for Angel, and loss for her husband, pulled apart her guts. These feelings were edged with her hatred for the scum that had kidnapped her. Louise knew that she would die before she let them lay a hand on her little daughter.

Ripped apart with emotion, Louise spent her time thinking of her husband—such thoughts, she knew, would keep her sane in the hell of isolation where they were being kept. Enforced isolation, a battle she had to fight.

But Mike's love helped her, just as it had during the years of war when he was long gone in the lost world of Vietnam. At that time she wondered whether he would live through that hell and return. He did. And that gave her strength.

Louise had been raised an army brat. She understood sacrifice and duty. She fully understood that those qualities made her husband such a special man. And *caring*. Michael was a caring man.

The lock mechanism clicked in the room's single door, slapping all comfort from Louise's mind. The door swung inward.

She rose to a sitting position on the edge of her bed. She worked hard at keeping the anxiety she felt off her face.

Angel continued to sleep on the bed beside her. The child was more than tired, she had reached the point of deep exhaustion.

Emilia Salerno walked in, briskly followed by two guards.

Louise felt a wave of nausea in her stomach. She let out a gasp. The woman held a pistol. She seemed to ignore the elder DiAlto.

Emilia pointed at the sleeping child, then snapped a command. One of the guards stepped forward and scooped up the little girl.

Louise leaped to her feet, panic exploding in her mind.

"No. No, please! You can't!"

Angel, awake now, looked over at her mother and screamed.

Louise flew blindly toward the guard holding her child. Emilia Salerno moved to cut her off.

Louise DiAlto felt a searing pain in the back of her head. A black blanket dropped over her senses.

GIA VALLONE, splayed out flat on a grassy knoll overlooking the Savasta palace, thought the ancestral estate looked peaceful, but she was not fooled by this temporary calm. It was the calm before the storm.

The big American had told her that in precisely four minutes, the estate would explode in hellfire and bloodshed.

Four minutes.

Gia watched from the Etruscan ruins. A white Fiat was parked behind her. She and the vehicle were out of sight of the palace that stood on lower ground beyond a stretch of vineyard. The anti-terrorist was armed with an Ingram autopistol, worn in a front-draw belt holster at her left hip. A Galil assault rifle was in the back seat of the Fiat.

She was hoping she would not have to use either—hers was supposed to be strictly a backup mission. She had been assigned a vital job, yes; but if the Americans were still under fire when they reached Gia's position, then there was little hope that the hostages they came to rescue would come out alive.

But if the battle zone did extend to where Gia was, she would not be afraid. She had journeyed near the edge where life met death many times, most recently in Bellagio. But she was afraid for Colonel Mike DiAlto and his wife and child. And, of course, she feared for the other two Americans.

Indeed, Gia felt more than compassion for Phoenix; she felt obligated to him. She knew she was close to death when he saved her in the early-morning hours at Bellagio. And for this she owed him, and owed him dearly.

The gutsy woman caught herself flicking a smile at her own thoughts. She would repay the American, she thought. Colonel John Phoenix was a most attractive man.

Gia understood the realities of her world and the world of a man like Phoenix. She knew he would be gone from her life within hours of the conclusion of this mission—and even that depended on whether they were both lucky enough to survive the battle ahead.

But, she thought, if they survived—even if they had only a heartbeat together—they could truly share that moment.

Now Gia Vallone channeled her thoughts away from Colonel John Phoenix. She had a job to do.

The latest terror in Tuscany was about to begin.

Three minutes.

19

ANTONIO MARTELLA could not believe his ears.

He had felt the DiAlto kidnapping assignment slipping out of his grasp ever since things went disastrously wrong in Bellagio. But at least he had remained in control of the situation.

But here was a lowly bodyguard pointing an accusing finger at him—CIA agent, my ass, he cursed to himself. The problem was that Viktor Karpov was seriously considering the accusation.

Antonio moved to clear himself. "It's a lie," he said. He tried to steady his rabbit-quick breathing. He looked from Leo Turrin and Nick the bodyguard across to the KGB man, whose authority far outweighed his own. "What proof do they have, Comrade Karpov? It is ridiculous."

"Not so goddamn ridiculous," Turrin growled. "You think my people don't have connections. They do. You were a guest of the CIA for a three-day briefing two months ago."

"A lie," repeated Martella, sweat beading on his forehead. "I have served the Column faithfully for three years. I stand behind my record!''

''Prove where you were from the fifteenth to seventeenth of February this year,'' Turrin demanded. ''You were in a safehouse being bought off by the CIA—you were out getting your goddamn goose cooked.''

''I...was on holiday,'' he replied. ''I was in Nice.''

''A *free* trip?'' Turrin asked sarcastically.

Antonio tried to speak, but could not. His throat was parched with dryness; his vocal cords were constricted with the tightness of fear. He knew they were setting him up. He knew they were professionals... the setup would have few, if any, holes.

He took a deep breath. He tried to compose himself. He realized one thing: Karpov believed them.

He pulled back a bit, trying to make the move seem natural. He kept his eyes on Karpov, but was still keenly aware of Turrin and the bodyguard. Nick was the most dangerous man in the room, that was obvious.

''I am trusted by my superiors in Rome,'' he said. ''The DiAlto kidnapping—it is my design.''

''Sure you engineered the kidnapping,'' Turrin said. ''Then you sold out.'' Leo turned to Karpov. ''Have your people run a check. I've got the Swiss bank account number. Antonio here made a small deposit of one hundred thousand American bones four days ago. It was his payoff for setting up the

Column. When the authorities close in on this joint, it's all over. And I'm willing to lay odds there's still plenty about the Column that he hasn't even told yet."

Karpov unleathered a silenced Walther PPK .380 automatic from under his loose suit. He held the weapon down at his side, pointed at the ground.

Martella knew he had to get his feet out of the grave. His fingertips drifted toward the butt of his Luger.

"It is easy for me to believe what you say," Karpov said to Turrin. "I have found this man's performance to be far less than satisfactory. The defection of Ciucci. The loss of the Vallone woman. The Bellagio disaster. The inability to control his troops, especially that bitch of a woman. But it would be dangerous for you, my American friend, if I were to learn that you speak in lies."

"It's the truth," snarled Nick the bodyguard.

Antonio Martella's nerves snapped under the pressure. His right hand clamped onto the butt of the Luger.

The Russian moved with well-trained speed. He shifted the Walther in a blurred target acquisition toward Antonio's forehead.

Martella had his Luger halfway from its holster, but Karpov was too fast for him.

A cry of protest caught in Martella's throat. The last thing he saw, save for the carpet that he landed on face-first, was a wink of flame emitted from the muzzle of Karpov's Walther.

This was not the first time Leo Turrin had seen Mack Bolan spring into action; it was, however, the fastest he had ever seen the big man move.

Bolan was about nine feet from Karpov. He brought up the Beretta in a two-fisted stance as the Russian turned to face him from aiming at Antonio.

Karpov saw death and there was no time to swing the Walther.

The Beretta spit flame that blew Karpov's left snake eye out of his head. The Russian crumpled to the floor. His movements, short and jerky, died with his nerves. The parabellum had bored through his head so fast it had left him like a puppet without strings. A wad of brain matter stained the wall behind where his head had been.

Leo went into a low crouch and panned the area with hawklike gaze and a smooth tracking motion of the .45.

Nothing moved.

"Looks all clear," Leo said. "Now what?"

Bolan gripped the briefcase packed with the fifty-grand payoff. He pitched the loot to Leo in an underhand toss.

"Go up on the roof and take this with you. Put it to good use. They'll be closing in on us from the wall anytime now."

Leo caught the briefcase. Both men started toward the archway leading into the depths of the castle.

The pair had always understood each other. It was a fighter's bond.

They were in a war together again, and actions were understood better than words.

20

Slivers of sunlight stabbed into the palace. A broad staircase arched upward. The stairs were carpeted, allowing for silent movement.

Bolan's pulse was pounding as he and Leo Turrin charged the staircase. Two commandos were heading down it.

Both men held Uzi machine guns. The Uzis looped down-and-under toward their prey. But the Americans had the split-second edge.

Bolan snapped off a round from the Beretta. A terrorist was tagged with a 9mm slap in the mouth, a slap that dropped the man in a dead heap.

Leo's .45 roared. A heavy round knocked the second man into a death-drop alongside his buddy.

The echo of the gunfire bounced madly off the tall walls of the hallway.

Bolan and Turrin grabbed the Uzis and extra ammo clips from the dead men.

The pair continued up the stairs. They stopped on the first level. They had to—they had been spotted by three men who stood midway down an arched corridor lined with closed doors.

The terrorist in the middle fell prone and opened fire. His two buddies backed off, then also opened fire. It was open season on Americans.

The Executioner flattened himself against the far wall. Turrin did the same against the closest wall.

Bolan heard the whine of death projectiles whipping around him, nailing walls and doors. He opened fire with the Uzi. Leo followed suit. Five weapons now hammered the corridor area.

Bolan scored the first hit, pegging the prone terrorist across his throat. The hardguy was nearly decapitated; his elbows collapsed and he fell across his smoking weapon.

One of the terrorists made a break for cover, provided behind one of the doors. He reached the handle, but Leo blasted him with a tight burst to the lower stomach and groin. He doubled over in death.

The surviving terrorist made a run for it. He had covered about five yards before Bolan triggered a burst from his Uzi. The man's arms flung out like a bird's wings as he was stitched in the back. His legs lost their power and he crashlanded on the floor.

Bolan glanced at Leo. The man's reflexes in battle remained in fine working order: Leo was unscathed.

The big warrior indicated the stairway.

"Keep going, Leo," he said.

"What about you?" Leo asked. "This place is a goddamn maze."

Before Bolan could reply, they heard a loud pounding sound. A man, near hysteria, was screaming from behind a closed door down the hall.

"Savasta," said Bolan. He glanced at his watch, then back at Leo. "Meet me at the car. If I'm not there in four minutes, go on your own."

"But...."

"Go," Bolan said.

"I'm gone, buddy. See you there."

Leo Turrin left the side of his fighting companion and continued up the stairway.

Bolan padded along the hallway to the door where the noise had sounded. Movement could be heard all over the palace; a large portion of the outside security force realized the attack had mushroomed from the inside. The Executioner knew one simple fact: time was scarce.

He had almost reached the door as two guards made a long turn around a corner. The hardguys ran toward Bolan and their own fate. The big guy fired a casual burst from the Uzi. The men crumpled.

He fed a fresh clip into the Uzi. With a powerful kick, he blasted open the door that separated him from the screams of a man who sounded like he was inches from the edge of madness. Bolan stalked inside with the Uzi up and ready.

All Bolan found was a middle-aged, pudgy man cringing in a corner. He was holding up his manicured hands as if to ward off death. He was screaming like a banshee.

"Senator," Bolan said.

"*Sí*...I am Senator Savasta! You must help me! Martella, he has ordered his men to shoot me on sight if I go outside this room!"

Bolan stood near the doorway. "Don't worry about Martella," he said. "Worry about me." To accent the statement, Bolan aimed the Uzi at Savasta's sizable gut.

The senator cringed, trying to crawl even farther into the corner. He was trying to burrow into the woodwork, and burrow out of the messy state he had placed himself in by helping Italy's vermin.

Shaking and stumbling over each word, the senator finally managed to voice his plea. "Please. No shoot. Please."

The big guy hated Savasta. He hated him for helping the terrorists, he hated him for being weak-kneed and he hated him for being reduced to such a squirming mass of flesh.

Bolan lifted the Uzi's muzzle and pointed it at the senator's sweating brow. "Where are the hostages, Senator? You can tell me now, or you can have a bullet in your head."

"At the end of the corridor! Go to your right! In the guest room, three doors down!"

The Executioner spun quickly and without comment. He was off down the corridor. He sensed that Savasta had stepped out of his room and was gazing after him.

"Signor!" the senator shouted. "What about me? Please don't leave me here in this prison. Please."

Bolan paused for a second just before the bend in the hallway. He tossed an indifferent look toward the pathetic senator. "Prison?" he questioned. "This is your home. *You* made it a prison."

"Signor," the senator pleaded. "What will happen to me?"

"You'll be shot on sight by Martella's forces. You're a marked man now, Senator. You're on your own."

The Executioner padded soundlessly around the corridor's main corner. He was about eight feet from the door where Savasta told him he would find Louise and Angel, when the door was pulled inward and a man's face emerged to investigate the noise.

The Uzi chattered with Bolan aiming and controlling its speech. The gun talked of death as it connected solidly. The guard toppled the rest of the way into the hallway, landing with a thump.

Bolan charged the doorway. A heartbeat before he reached it, he propelled himself forward into a somersault that threw him into the room at a low level, below the range of gunfire that immediately opened up.

He came out of the roll with his back to the wall, his Uzi tracking. He took in the scene with a snap scan.

Five people were in the spacious room. The furniture had been cleared to the sides. All that remained in the middle of the room was an old cot.

A hardguy was tracking a machine pistol for another shot in the Executioner's direction.

Another male terrorist was holding something. The something was squirming and making a hellish screaming noise. It was Angel DiAlto.

Emilia Salerno stood beside the terrorist. Louise DiAlto lay limp on the floor at their feet. Salerno held the child's tiny wrist in one hand. Her other hand held a scalpel that reflected the overhead light.

Emilia looked up at the cause of the sudden interruption. The scalpel was poised just inches above one of Angel's tiny fingers.

Time stood still. The picture froze in the Executioner's mind.

He fired a burst at the terrorist with the machine pistol. The guy received hot lead in the region of his heart. He fell over his own numbed feet and collapsed to the floor in a puddle of death.

Emilia and the terrorist beside her responded in the only way Bolan could have hoped for: they reached for their weapons and ignored the child. Bolan knew that if either of the terrorists had stuck a gun to

Angel's head, the hit would have been over and the terrorists could have claimed victory.

Emilia started to yank the Scorpion from its holster.

The man who held Angel fell away from Emilia. He dropped the child to the floor and pawed for a 9mm Beretta worn in an exposed shoulder holster. He had time to shout, but that was all. He had no time to dodge the bullets that blasted his face. There was little left of that face when he hit the floor.

Emilia completed the fast-draw that cleared the Scorpion from its holster. She felt sudden agony. Slugs flattened her back against the wall, ruining expensive wallpaper with blood. She took one, two stumbling steps toward Bolan, hate firing in her eyes. The big guy fed the last of the appropriated ammo clips into the smoking Uzi. But he did not need them.

Emilia Salerno splashed onto the carpet. Gone was one of the most ruthless bitches Bolan had ever encountered.

Angel, her face stricken with horror, was crying. The child was crying for her mother, for her father and for herself.

Bolan stepped across the dead bodies.

He took a closer look at Louise. The mother was unconscious, but alive. She had a bloodied bump on the back of her head.

She did not regain consciousness when Bolan lifted her over his shoulder in a fireman's carry. Just as well, he thought. The warrior then moved over to the trembling girl.

"Angel," he said, his voice a soft, soothing whisper. "Your father sent me here to get you. I'm going to take you home."

Two words sparked the girl's attention: *father* and *home*. More than anything, at that moment, little Angel DiAlto wanted to see her father and she wanted to be home.

The young girl looked at her mother, slung over Bolan's shoulder. "Is mommy okay?"

"She's fine, Angel. And we're going to get her home, too. You've got to be real quiet though, okay?"

She nodded.

The Executioner lifted the child and gave her his left hip to ride on.

He hit the hallway in a run, retracing his steps. He had only two minutes left to get back to Leo, or else his friend would be off without him.

He reached the landing of the staircase. He could feel Louise's breath. Angel clung to him. He started down the stairs.

A terrorist approached the bottom step. The guncock carried an AK assault rifle. He was charging to back up Emilia and her crew. He never made the first step. Bolan, despite his burden, held the folding stock of the Uzi close against his side. He triggered a death rattle that riddled the bastard from stomach to chin.

He reached the bottom of the stairs and angled in the direction of the parking area beside the castle.

The Lancia was out there.

So was the enemy.

The Lancia he would welcome; the enemy he would kill.

21

BOLAN PAUSED WHEN he reached the archway leading to the parking lot. He surveyed the scene alongside the ancestral home of Gaspare Savasta.

The Lancia, looking proud and powerful, stood where Bolan had parked it when he and Leo first arrived.

In addition to the half dozen other vehicles that occupied the blacktopped square, the Executioner could see eight figures wearing the uniform of the Red Justice Column. Two of the hardguys were running away from Bolan, heading to secure another palace exit. Six terrorists were only five hundred feet away and closing fast.

The outside security forces, drawn in from the perimeter, had not yet seen Bolan. But it was only a matter of time.

With Louise and Angel riding him like a train, Bolan's mobility was severely hindered and his chances cut by half.

At that moment, Leo Turrin did his thing from above. From two stories overhead, Leo put the fifty thousand dollars to good use, just as Bolan had instructed.

The Red Justice Column guards were suddenly aware of one-hundred-dollar bills floating down like a green shower. They recognized the American money. They recognized their good fortune. They stopped everything.

Bolan used the distraction to make his move. He broke from the house, the Uzi firing in his grip. As he ran he heard the sound of another Uzi chipping in. Leo was again at work.

Some terrorists had already bent over to examine the bills and had begun picking them up. A few others merely stood looking skyward at the raining greenbacks.

Only two men were smart enough to keep their attention on the palace. Bolan took these two out first. The Executioner and the Uzi blazed forward.

Reaching the Lancia, he turned to look back and saw three Red Column commandos wasted on the parking tarmac, felled by Leo's covering fire.

Leo stopped shooting. Bolan knew his companion was on his way back downstairs. He heard an automatic fire from inside the palace. It was answered by a single shot. The automatic weapon did not repeat its call. Bolan knew that Leo was okay, but a guard was not.

Stooping behind the Lancia, Bolan was under fire from three guncocks. Their rounds were bouncing

off and around the car. The big guy set Louise
DiAlto down on the ground, her back resting against
one of the tires. Her eyelids fluttered. She was coming to, Bolan realized, as he rested Angel in her lap.

Doing the unexpected to keep the terrorists off
guard, the Executioner dived away from the car, rolling in a quick tumble. He halted in a splay-legged
crouch.

He sent a blistering figure eight of lead at the three
men. Grunts and squeals of pain followed the round.
Three figures shuddered as death grabbed them.

Seeing no other terrorists posing an immediate
threat, Bolan returned to Louise and Angel. The
mother was now awake, her eyes sparkling.

"Thank you," she said, her voice sounding worn
yet sincere.

"We're not out of it yet," he snapped. "You and
Angel get in the back seat. Stay down as low as you
can get."

The pair nodded, then carried out the big guy's
orders.

Bolan continued to scan the area, his eyes working
like radar. He quickly slipped in behind the Lancia's
steering wheel. He cranked the ignition. The engine
turned over, caught and gunned to life.

He backed the Lancia into a sharp turn. The car
was waiting at the archway when Leo Turrin came
hustling outside. He hopped into the front bucket
seat next to Bolan.

The Executioner rammed the Lancia into gear. The nose of the car lifted, and the machine roared down the road leading toward the front gate of the palace grounds.

Bolan heard the sounds of a helicopter—the Bell UH-D he had seen earlier—revving up behind the palace. When the driveway cut away from the structure, he risked a quick glance over his shoulder. He caught a glimpse of the helicopter lifting off from its pad.

The Lancia was bearing down on the main gate.

"Ready?" he asked Turrin.

"Ready," Turrin replied.

Bolan yanked the steering wheel to the left. The Lancia skidded smoothly into a sideways slide, sending up a shower of dust and gravel, slowing to a stop.

Three guards were standing post, waiting for this moment. The gunmen prepared to open fire on the car.

Two of the guards were kneeling in the middle of the driveway. The third sentry began firing from the doorway of the guardhouse.

Leo Turrin triggered his Uzi from the open window on his side of the car. A line of holes traced a pattern across the face of the guardhouse, and across the face of the guard there. The man dropped to the ground, where he died like a doormat of death.

Bolan leaped from the driver's side of the vehicle. He steadied his Uzi over the Lancia's roof and opened fire at the two men blocking the roadway. He felt one of their bullets breeze past his cheek.

He finished off the Uzi's clip on the sentries.

As the slugs connected, Bolan heard the sound of the helicopter rising to a low hover behind the building. Bolan turned from the riddled bodies and looked back at the copter. It was moving in their direction. He also saw a small truck that held the remaining gunmen of Antonio Martella's Red Justice Column unit.

The Executioner knew it was time for an exit—and a fast one. He ran to the gatehouse and stepped over the dead guard. Quickly he reached inside and activated the mechanism that opened the gate.

Racing back to the car, the warrior discarded the empty Uzi. He piled in behind the steering wheel and floored the Lancia. The car rocketed through the main gate.

Bolan wheeled to their left. The Etruscan ruins were three-quarters of a mile to the north, and that's where Bolan was heading.

The Lancia fishtailed wildly out of the high-speed turn. He put the gas pedal down as the vehicle put yardage between itself and the gate.

The helicopter swung out over the walls of the palace grounds. Bolan heard the big bird swooping down at them.

"Hold on," he growled to his passengers.

He commenced steering in a drunken pattern,

wheeling the vehicle from shoulder to shoulder on the dirt road. The Lancia skidded as if on ice. Bolan locked his fists around the steering wheel as the car vibrated violently from its wild journey.

The sound of automatic-weapon fire began as it opened up from the chopper. Twin lines of spurting dirt tracked the swerving vehicle.

Rounds snapped into the tail of the Lancia. Another sharp twist of the steering wheel took the car out of the line of fire.

The Etruscan ruins were ahead on the right.

Gia should be there. Gia Vallone *would* be there.

The chopper continued to play tag with the Lancia.

Then the battle dam broke open.

Bolan steered the Lancia into another tight swerve that sent the car bumping onto the rutted path that led to the ruins.

And from the ruins a weapon report sounded. It led to a booming response. A tremendous explosion in the air rocked the hellgrounds.

Bolan braked the vehicle to a stop. He climbed out of the Lancia just in time to see the helicopter falling from the sky, a blossoming flower of flames and smoke.

The Executioner palmed his Beretta.

Gia Vallone stood in the clearing behind the Etruscan site, out of sight of the road. She gripped the Galil assault rifle. She had brought down the chopper with the Galil on grenade-launcher mode.

"Bring your car over here," Bolan yelled, waving to Gia. "I've got some passengers for you."

The woman disappeared behind the crumbling walls of the Etruscan site. She returned driving a Fiat. As the car pulled alongside the Lancia, Bolan opened the back door of his car.

Louise and Angel DiAlto, crouching as low as possible, slid into the back seat of the Fiat.

"You're almost in the clear now," Bolan told them. "Go with Gia. She'll take you to meet someone you might just want to see—Mike." Bolan then turned his attention to his longtime companion, Leo Turrin. "Leo, you head out with them."

"But. . . ."

Bolan cut Leo off before he could get going on a long-winded sentence. Give Leo a chance, and he could talk anyone into anything.

"They may need you, Leo," he said.

Turrin nodded.

Gia kept the Fiat at low idle. Her brown eyes took a thirsty drink of Bolan before she spoke. "Now I have saved *your* life, Colonel Phoenix. Now we are equals."

Bolan reached into the seat beside Gia and yanked out the Galil and a grenade that lay beside it.

"Thanks for what you did, Gia. But it didn't change your status at all—we were always equals."

The Executioner then slapped the roof of the Fiat.

"On your way," he said.

Gia goosed the gas and pulled away from the ruins in a swirl of gravel and dust. Bolan watched them go: Gia and Leo in the front, Louise and Angel in the back. The big guy felt good. Damn good.

He really respected Leo for following his instructions even though, Bolan knew, it tore him up to leave the scene of action. Leo had been a very necessary element in the key that had unlocked the DiAltos from the prison. But Bolan felt he could no longer endanger the life of such an important undercover operative in the U.S. government's continuing war on organized crime. Too much work and too many years had gone into placing Leo on *La Commissióne* for it all to be lost in a battle at Tuscany.

Besides, this was one road Mack Bolan knew he should travel alone.

The Executioner loaded the fragmentation grenade into the assault rifle's launcher device. He then turned and carried the Galil up an incline that crested in a natural overlook above the road leading to the Savasta palace.

The truck he had seen while still on the estate was lumbering in pursuit along the road below Bolan's position.

The Executioner sighted on the truck. He made allowance for distance and wind. Then he firmly stroked the Galil's trigger.

He was still riding the rifle's recoil when a flash engulfed the truck.

The metal box that had been the terrorists' last-hope vehicle came to a halt in crackling flames. The smell of charred clothing and burning flesh drifted with the breeze. And nothing moved. Nothing but Bolan.

The Executioner slowly made his way back to the Lancia. He crawled in behind the wheel and placed the assault rifle on the front seat next to him.

He wheeled the car around and followed the same route taken earlier by Gia Vallone.

He had given his all.

He was exhausted.

But he was not beyond a grim smile.

The money that had floated down on the terrorists, delaying the departure of the pursuit truck whose gutted hulk sat in the road behind him, had been fake.

Fifty thousand dollars of confiscated counterfeit had bamboozled a venal enemy into making its last mistake.

Sure, money was tight nowadays, and harder than ever to come by. But action—The Executioner's kind of action—was available for as long as the big guy lived.

So the money they could fake.

But the action—that was for real, every time.

22

MACK BOLAN, once again back in his role as Colonel John Phoenix, witnessed the reunion of the DiAlto family at a NOCS field office in Florence. Relief and happiness, raw emotion, filled the scene.

Bolan stood back, watching from the sidelines as a spectator. Alongside the big American stood Gia Vallone.

The pair watched as Mike DiAlto hugged his wife and daughter. Mike DiAlto had done his job, now he was being rewarded.

Colonel DiAlto had attended to Vianake in a professional manner while Bolan and Turrin blitzed the terrorists in Tuscany.

Bolan's hunch and DiAlto's surveillance had paid off. Paid off big.

Captain Vianake started losing his backbone after Bolan and company survived the mortar attack in Milan. Like an idiot, Vianake tried to contact the Red Justice Column. The Column would have nothing to do with him; they left him alone, on his own, to rot.

Mike DiAlto, however, would not leave the fink

alone. He closed in on Vianake, collected enough evidence then confronted the captain. Guns went off. One man died. It was not Mike DiAlto.

Leo Turrin was absent at the DiAlto reunion. Leo was already aboard a commercial flight to the *La Commissióne* boardroom in New York. The highly placed undercover Fed was on his way back to the tightrope he walked every day of his life.

Gia Vallone had greeted Bolan with word that Gaspare Savasta had managed to escape from the home that he had turned into a prison. The senator had turned himself in, to save his life, and he was singing to anyone who would listen about the activities of the Red Justice Column.

Bolan kept his eyes on the DiAltos. As the family turned to quit the scene, the Executioner felt a twinge of emotion pulling at his gut. The feeling was for home. The big guy wanted to be back on his native soil.

Mack Bolan, victorious in his Italian mission, wanted to be back with the ones he loved: his associates and friends at Stony Man Farm.

Taking a long, loving look at Gia Vallone, the warrior said: "You're a good woman, Gia. And a helluva fighter. Take care."

"Kiss me, dammit," came the accented reply.

She was smiling, near him at last. Close to his soul.

He kissed her deeply, in gratitude.

Then Mack Bolan headed home.

EPILOGUE

THE EXECUTIONER had fought and bled and put his powerful body through the stresses of hell so that others would not have to.

He and his allies waded step by step through hellfire and destruction so that other men could live in peace.

The future could not, under any circumstances, be entrusted to the likes of the Red Justice Column.

Mack Bolan had meted out quick and final judgment with a .44 AutoMag, a Beretta and a tightly clasped Uzi because death was the only punishment that the ghoulish predators he fought against could understand.

A skull blown bloodily apart...a .44 Magnum slug in the guts...a choked scream ripped from a throat torn by a jacketed 9mm bullet—his guns spoke the only language the enemy comprehended without a translator.

Death was what they understood.

Mack Bolan had spoken their language perfectly.

And yet the big guy hoped that he would finally be

measured not by the lives he had taken, the men he had killed, but by the vastly greater number of good humans who were able to live out their lives in peace because of Mack Bolan's work.

They were the good souls who went about their daily lives in quiet and serenity, never aware of the unending war against evil that Mack Bolan waged. They lived easy because the man with the steel eyes and determined heart lived hard. They would never know the hell he put himself through, or the tortures of each last mile.

There were still more miles to be walked, more journeys through danger and death to be made. And there was no one but The Executioner to make them.

He'd make them the same way he had made all the other last miles—one by one, each with a burning anger at the terror merchants who preyed on the weak of the world, each with his senses honed to the utmost.

Mack Bolan's business was execution.

He would do it right. He knew no other way. He would do it until it killed him.

For us.

"I am known as the vulture's vengeance. By death I come to life. But to those good others I say: take a stand. Feed the hungry. Clothe the naked. Care for the sick.

"Don't die in the middle. Live large."

The Guns
of
Colonel John Phoenix

Beretta 93-R

An advanced self-loading pistol, the 93-R can fire either single shots or three-round bursts. For distant or difficult shots, a small front handgrip folds down for the left hand; left thumb hooks through extended trigger guard for extra control. Folding carbine stock can be clipped onto butt for shoulder firing, transforming an apparently ordinary self-loading pistol into a deadly accurate machine pistol.

Fires 9mm parabellum rounds; short recoil operation, hinged block locking. Detachable box magazine, 15 or 20 rounds. Achieves muzzle velocity of 375 meters per second.* With 15-round box and carbine metal stock, the 93-R weighs 1.39 kg. Length of gun minus stock, 240mm. Rate of fire: 110 rounds per minute.

Modified for Mack Bolan with suppressor and specially machined springs designed to cycle subsonic cartridges, effectively silencing the weapon. Flash-hider for night firing. The 93-R eliminates opponents precisely, silently and invisibly.

* *The specifications for the following weaponry are provided by the manufacturers and therefore vary, in some instances being metric and in others imperial.*

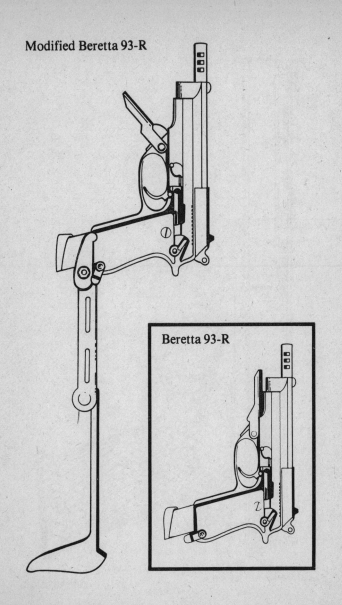

Modified Beretta 93-R

Beretta 93-R

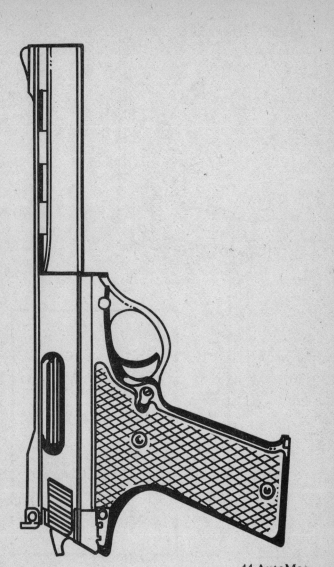

.44 AutoMag

.44 AutoMag

''The Flesh Shredder.'' Automatic handgun of impressive size, weight and recoil. Gun designed around a wildcat cartridge, the .44 Auto Magnum, produced by marrying a .44 revolver bullet with a cut-down 7.62mm NATO rifle cartridge case.

A recoil-operated pistol with a rotating bolt head controlled by cam tracks in the pistol frame, the series C AutoMag fires a 240-grain bullet at a muzzle velocity of 1,640 feet per second with muzzle energy of 1,455 lbs. Requires a bolt with six locking lugs to contain explosive internal gas pressures.

Its 6.5-inch barrel makes the AutoMag 11.5 inches in length. Unloaded, it weighs almost four pounds. A silver monster, the AutoMag is as close to a rifle as any handgun can be. Massive recoil demands powerful grasp. Its 240-grain boattail slug can tear through the solid metal of an automobile engine block.

Uzi Submachine Gun

Developed by the Israeli army in the early fifties, the Uzi is modeled mainly on the Czech Models 23 and 25 submachine guns. This blowback weapon has an overhung bolt, reducing the length of the gun to 470mm with its metal butt folded, and only 640mm with butt extended for accurate firing from the shoulder. A 32-round magazine enters the pistol grip, increasing magazine rigidity and making reloading in darkness easier. To increase firepower, two magazines are welded together at right angles: when both are full, one extends forward under and parallel to the barrel; when one is empty, it extends backward. Added magazine increases weight at the front of the gun to prevent muzzle climb during auto firing.

Body is strengthened by the formation of fullering grooves, which make it easier to handle in adverse operating conditions. Intelligent use of sheet-metal stampings and plastics results in weight of 3.5 kg. Barrel rifling: 4 grooves RH, 1 turn in 245mm. Firing 600 9mm parabellum rounds per minute, the gun is capable of unleashing a full magazine in just over three seconds, at a muzzle velocity of 420 meters per second. Effective range: 200 meters. Mack Bolan's Uzi is modified with flash-hider for undetected night firing.

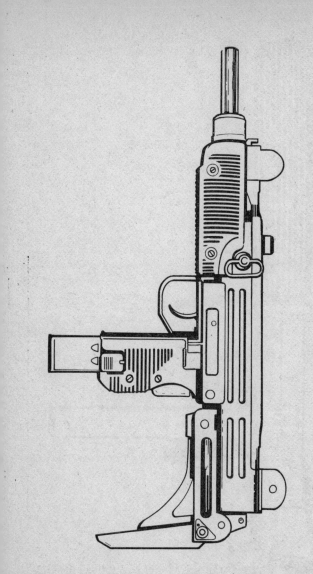

Uzi Submachine Gun

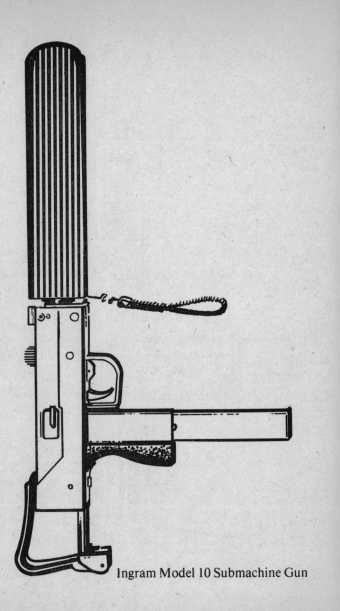

Ingram Model 10 Submachine Gun

Ingram Model 10 Submachine Gun

Very short, very compact SMG. Bolan's latest model is chambered for .45 ACP rounds in 30-round magazine. Uses stamped metal components, an overhung bolt of sheet steel weighted with lead, and barrel threaded to take suppressor. Easily concealed.

Weight when empty: 2.84 kg; loaded with 30 rounds .45 ACP, 3.82 kg. Length with telescoped stock 269mm. Barrel length 146mm. Suppressor weighs .545 kg, and is 291mm long. Barrel rifling: 6 grooves RH; for .45 ACP rounds, 1 turn in 508mm. Muzzle velocity: 280 meters per second with .45 ACP, at a cyclic rate of 1,145 rounds per minute.

Bolan uses MAC suppressor. The MAC reduces emergent gas velocity to subsonic level. Target hears only the crack that the bullet carries with it. Suppressor tube covered with Nomex-A heat-resistant material. Also comes with long barrel for increased range and improved bullet power.

Wraparound bolt keeps the center of gravity over the pistol grip for steady one-handed firing. Compact, close-range weapon can deliver decimating firepower in quiet but potent bursts.

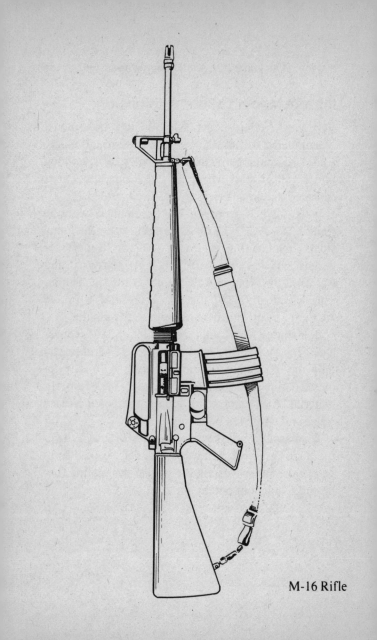

M-16 Rifle

M-16 Rifle

This Vietnam veteran fires a 5.56mm caliber cartridge at high velocity, can puncture an army helmet at 500 meters. A lightweight, low-impulse rifle, the M-16 weighs 3.1 kgs. Gas direct-fire operation using a rotating bolt lock. Uses 20- or 30-round magazine.

Rounds use tubular IMR propellant. Buffer modified to control rate of fire. Chamber is chromium-plated.

M-16 with sling and loaded 30-round magazine weighs only 3.73 kg. Trigger pull: 2.3–3.8kp. Length with flash suppressor 990mm, barrel 508mm. Barrel rifling: 6 grooves RH, one turn in 305mm. Muzzle velocity 1000 meters per second. Cyclic firing rate between 700 and 950 rounds per minute. Effective range: 400 meters.

A lightweight supermodern automatic rifle, the M-16's controversial handling qualities make it a deadly weapon for a wide range of clandestine operations.

M-203 Grenade Launcher

Developed under the direction of United States Army Weapons Command, the lightweight M-203 is a single-shot, breech-loaded, pump action grenade launcher fired from the shoulder. Bolan's is more often than not attached to the underside of the M-16.

Length 394mm, weight loaded 1.63 kg, combined weight with the M-16 is 5 kg. A 40mm grenade round achieves muzzle velocity of 71 meters per second. Range: 400 meters. Effective range for area targets 350 meters; point target 150 meters.

Ammo types: high explosive, air burst, smokeless and flashless. High-explosive round contains a grenade 38mm in diameter with 35g of explosive. Formed of rectangular-wrapped steel wire, notched to allow fragmentation.

The M-203 transforms the M-16 automatic rifle into a highly mobile single-piece destruction unit.

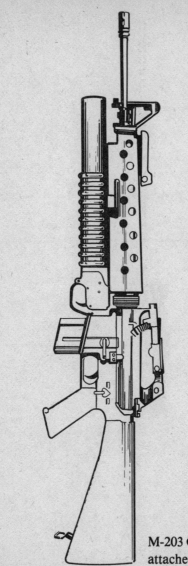

M-203 Grenade Launcher
attached to M-16

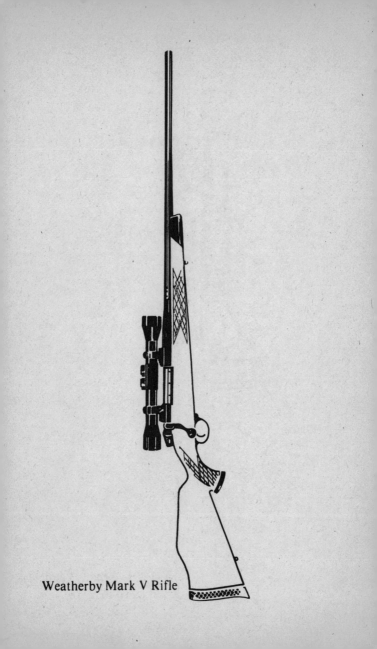

Weatherby Mark V Rifle

Weatherby Mark V Rifle

Bolt-action .460 Magnum hunting rifle. Developed by Roy Weatherby, whose theories on ballistics (involving light, high-velocity bullets) revolutionized big-game hunting. Five-hundred-grain bullet achieves highest velocity of any bullet in the world. A monster in both power and size, with a 26-inch chrome-lined barrel and overall length of 46.5 inches, the Mark V is short of four feet long and weighs 10.5 lbs. Bolt sleeve enclosed from the rear; incredibly strong action made entirely from steel, no alloy parts. Streamlined action weighs only 36 oz. Shotgun-type buttplate with ventilated rubber recoil pad to handle the 100 lbs. of free recoil.

Nondetachable staggered box magazine holds two shots. Achieves muzzle velocity of 2,700 feet per second, 2,300 fps at 100 yards, 2,005 fps at 200 yards, 1,730 fps at 300 yards. Energy at muzzle is a thundering 8,095 foot-pounds, 6,025 at 100 yards, 4,465 at 200 yards, 3,320 at 300 yards. Midrange trajectory at 100 yards: +0.7 inches.

High-powered hunting rifle with massive stopping power, wielded by the strongest shootists only.

A last word on the Beretta 93-R from Andrjez Konzaki

"The 93-R is a new design from Beretta that I have been working on for Mack, following my work on the less advanced 92-S. Beretta insists that only an armorer can strip the exquisite burst-control mechanism at this stage of the development. We think we're getting the very best use it is possible to get out of a 93-R, and it is a remarkable piece. It's a machine pistol that can be carried and used in the same way as a single-handed pistol. It can be fired just like any other pistol, but for hits beyond normal pistol range or for tricky shots at close range, the forehand grip folded down provides a controlled two-handed aim that is steadier by far than the TV-cop-show method of clasping the butt with two hands. This is a most exciting addition to the Stony Man armory, has proven itself well and is in the forefront of a variety of new weapons—Carl Lyons's Atchisson, the bazooka I'm cooking up for Phoenix Force, some underbelly firepower for Jack Grimaldi—that we are developing in live engagement and on the bench to guarantee Stony Man combat superiority.''

MACK BOLAN

THE EXECUTIONER 53

BOLAN

appears again in
The Invisible Assassins

An American computer expert is cut down on a dark street in front of Mack Bolan's eyes.

Within hours The Executioner is on his way to Japan, where he faces fanatical hatreds keener than a swordblade. Alone in an alien land, he wages fierce war to prevent the most hideous secret of World War II from triggering a final act of madness.

In THE INVISIBLE ASSASSINS Bolan takes on the *Yakuza*, a gangster organization as powerful as his Mafia enemies of the past. All hell bursts loose when the ace dealer of death takes his new war to the land of the rising sun....

Available wherever paperbacks are sold.

An excerpt from
STONY MAN DOCTRINE

BARRELING THROUGH THE FLAMING trucks and diesel
smoke, Mack Bolan put single shots into terrorists.
Rocket after rocket hit the trucks, killing concealed
hardguys and gutting the fiery hulks.

A soldier broke cover and sprinted for the rocks.
Suddenly he fell. Bolan sighted on the guy's head,
but he did not fire.

Through the scope, Bolan watched as the guy
clutched at his throat and started to thrash. Finally
he died, froth bubbling from his mouth.

A green cloud obscured Bolan's field of view.
Out of the corner of his eye he saw a man in an
anticontamination suit. Bolan followed him with the
scope. He saw that the guy wore a gas mask and a
plastic hood.

Gas!

Yellow rain in Laos and Cambodia, chemicals of
mass murder in Afghanistan. Why not poison gas in
the Americas?

Bolan keyed his radio, yelled into it. "Get back!
That's gas over there. Poison gas. Pull back. Pull
back now!"

MACK BOLAN

THE EXECUTIONER SERIES

Bolan took the lady by the arm and escorted her out of there, telling the enemy at the door, "Stay put, we'll be right back."

As they crossed the mercenary compound toward the lab building, she whisperingly marveled, "You just tell them what to do and they do it, huh?"

"Sure. First thing a soldier learns is to obey. These are good soldiers."

He did not discourage the quiet exchange; it made them seem more natural in this dangerous place. The girl shivered and moved closer to him. "But they're not for real."

"Oh, they're for real," he assured her. "As good as you'll find anywhere."

"I think it's horrible," she said. She shivered again and moved just a little bit away. "I saw you kill tonight," she confided.

"That's okay," he said soberly. "I saw you try to kill tonight, and I was on the deadly end of it."

"That was different," she protested.

"It's different every time," he told her.

—*The Executioner #45*
Paramilitary Plot

Mack Bolan is unbeatable! In the excerpt quoted, Bolan's luminous approach to the savage pastures shines through like a beacon for the burdened and the oppressed. The continuing terrorist wars are The Executioner's opportunity to attack civilization's enemies like no other hero in history. Stony Man One, also known as John Phoenix, has become a new kind of mighty avenger whose enemies, as prophesied, ''shall lick the dust!''

These are hard times we live in, and the free world has never before been in such need of a man like John Phoenix. We are threatened on all sides by escalating degrees of savagery and terror, and only one blitzer—backed by his superlative allies—is prepared at all times to meet vicious danger head-on.

Mack Bolan's transformation into the magnificent John Phoenix has been chronicled in a series of gut-chilling stories that have become major publishing events.

Executioner #47: Renegade Agent is a brilliant and complex story about Bolan's confrontation with good guys gone bad—a turncoat CIA agent and a treacherous British double agent. Mack gets them both, in a rain of hellfire that takes out their sidekicks, too.

Executioner #48: The Libya Connection presents Bolan with one of the worst atrocities he had ever faced, and the pain is so great for this good man that his campaign against terror is recharged, and his commitment to crush evil is redoubled.

Executioner #49: Doomsday Disciples is a searing tale told at white heat about a KGB-controlled cult in San Francisco, a story of wholesale butchery that is only a heartbeat away from today's headlines.

Executioner #50: Brothers in Blood has a survivalist flavor as Mack Bolan takes to the woods to purge body and soul of fatigue. But there are killers wherever he goes, and Bolan has no choice but to wrench the gun barrels of terror around and let the aggressors take a long, slow look into their black depths.

Executioner #51: Vulture's Vengeance brings Bolan and flyboy ally Jack Grimaldi together in a soaring adventure that takes them fifteen miles above the surface of the earth, as they prepare to tear into the heart of a savage kidnap-and-assassination plot.

Executioner #52: Tuscany Terror is published at a time when the Rand Corporation's Security and Subnational Conflict Program indicates that world terrorism is setting new records, with attacks on American officials abroad increased by fifty percent. Acting on evidence that foreign backing for both leftist and rightist terrorists in Italy is part of a plot to destabilize that key NATO country, Italian police have arrested terrorist suspects from Libya, Lebanon, Bulgaria and West Germany. Authorities have been confounded and their intelligence resources totally consumed by the kidnapping of U.S. General James L. Dozier, and a West German terror-gang's rocket assault on the car of U.S. General Frederick Kroesen. The country is still enmeshed in the sinister international implications of the plot to assassinate the Pope. The time is always right for Mack Bolan!

Coming in future months are more stirring Mack Bolan stories set in Japan, the Colorado Rockies, Maine, Central Africa, then back to Europe with Mack's new Laser Wagon.

The hydra-headed enemy needs chopping at every turn. It is a challenge The Executioner accepts with grim determination. In his new war he has fought alongside familiar friends—Toby Ranger, Leo Turrin, Tommy Anders—and he has known new allies—Tran Le, Holly Bruce, Johnny Kerr, Gia Vallone....

Soon he faces his greatest challenge yet, against a troika of terror in a "SuperAdventure" novel entitled *Stony Man Doctrine*. This is a flaming story of raw courage and nerves-of-steel action in which Bolan at last teams up with Phoenix Force and Able Team. Watch for it! It will be one of the great peaks in action-adventure publishing.

Meanwhile, the Executioner series PHOENIX FORCE, by Gar Wilson, and ABLE TEAM, by Dick Stivers, confirm Gold Eagle's position at the forefront of the genre. Don Pendleton calls Dick Stivers "brilliant." *Marketing Bestsellers* says Gar Wilson's books are "making history—strong-willed and true!" Watch for these books wherever The Executioner is sold. They are *all* unbeatable!

> "The Executioner series has improved immensely. Bookstores have a hard time keeping it in stock. This is a publishing marvel that will be around a long time!"
>
> *The Orlando Voice*

MACK BOLAN

THE EXECUTIONER SERIES

I am not their judge. I am their judgment—I am their executioner.
— *Mack Bolan,*
a.k.a. Col. John Phoenix

Mack Bolan is the free world's leading force in the new Terrorist Wars, defying all terrorists and destroying them piece by piece, using his Vietnam-trained tactics and knowledge of jungle warfare. Bolan's new war is the most exciting series ever to explode into print. You won't want to miss a single word. Start your collection now!

GOLD EAGLE

Available wherever paperbacks are sold.

Mack Bolan's

PHOENIX FORCE

AN EXECUTIONER SERIES

by Gar Wilson

Phoenix Force is The Executioner's five-man army
that blazes through the dirtiest of encounters. Like
commandos who fight for the love of battle and the
righteous unfolding of the logic of war, Bolan's five
hardasses make mincemeat out of their enemies.
Catch up on the whole series now!

"Strong-willed and true. Gold Eagle Books are
making history. Full of adventure, daring and
action!"

—*Marketing Bestsellers*

#1 Argentine Deadline   **#4 Tigers of Justice**
#2 Guerilla Games   **#5 The Fury Bombs**
#3 Atlantic Scramble

Phoenix Force titles are available
wherever paperbacks are sold.

GOLD EAGLE

Mack Bolan's

ABLE TEAM

AN EXECUTIONER SERIES

by Dick Stivers

In the fire-raking tradition of The Executioner, Able Team's Carl Lyons, Pol Blancanales and Gadgets Schwarz are the three hotshots who avenge terror with screaming silvered fury. They are the Death Squad reborn, and their long-awaited adventures are the best thing to happen since the Mack Bolan and the Phoenix Force series. Collect them all! They are classics of their kind! Do not miss these titles:

"Written in the inimitable Executioner style!"
—*Mystery News*

#1 Tower of Terror   #4 Amazon Slaughter
#2 The Hostaged Island   #5 Cairo Countdown
#3 Texas Showdown   #6 Warlord of Azatlan

Able Team titles are available
wherever paperbacks are sold.

GOLD EAGLE

BOLAN FIGHTS AGAINST ALL ODDS TO DEFEND FREEDOM!

Mail this coupon today!

Gold Eagle Reader Service, a division of Worldwide Library
In U.S.A.: 2504 W. Southern Avenue, Tempe, Arizona 85282
In Canada: 649 Ontario Street, Stratford, Ontario N5A 6W2

FREE! MACK BOLAN BUMPER STICKER
when you join our home subscription plan.

YES. please send me my first four Executioner novels. and include my FREE Mack Bolan bumper sticker as a gift. These first four books are mine to examine free for 10 days. If I am not entirely satisfied with these books. I will return them within 10 days and owe nothing. If I decide to keep these novels. I will pay just $1.95 per book (total $7.80). I will then receive the four new Executioner novels every other month as soon as they come off the presses. and will be billed the same low price of $7.80 per shipment. I understand that each shipment will contain two Mack Bolan novels. one Able Team and one Phoenix Force. There are no shipping and handling or any other hidden charges. I may cancel this arrangement at any time. and the bumper sticker is mine to keep as a FREE gift. even if I do not buy any additional books.

NAME _____ (PLEASE PRINT)

ADDRESS _____ APT. NO.

CITY _____ STATE/PROV. _____ ZIP/POSTAL CODE

Signature _____ (If under 18. parent or guardian must sign.)

This offer limited to one order per household. We reserve the right to exercise discretion in granting membership. If price changes are necessary. you will be notified. Offer expires September 30. 1983

166-BPM-PABB